"You're not a coward," Paul said and placed his hand over hers.

"You were surviving. And if you hadn't put it all out of your mind, he would have come after you before now. Before you were better prepared to deal with it."

Ginny gave him a small smile. "Before you were here to help me."

Paul squeezed her hand. "We're going to get through this, and then your life can be about the future and not the past."

The future.

Paul's words hung in the air as if to tease her with possibilities that she knew would never be. She raised her gaze to his and realized just how close to her he was. He leaned in to kiss her and her body responded before her mind could put on the brakes.

JANA DeLEON

THE LOST GIRLS OF JOHNSON'S BAYOU

TORONTO NEW YORK LONDON
AMSTERDAM PARIS SYDNEY HAMBURG
STOCKHOLM ATHENS TOKYO MILAN MADRID
PRAGUE WARSAW BUDAPEST AUCKLAND

To my mentor and friend, Jane Graves, for being so willing to share all your knowledge with a rank beginner.

Recycling programs
for this product may
not exist in your area.

ISBN-13: 978-0-373-69598-0

THE LOST GIRLS OF JOHNSON'S BAYOU

Copyright © 2012 by Jana DeLeon

ABOUT THE AUTHOR

Jana DeLeon grew up among the bayous and small towns of southwest Louisiana. She's never actually found a dead body or seen a ghost, but she's still hoping. Jana started writing in 2001 and focuses on murderous plots set deep in the Louisiana bayous. By day, she writes very boring technical manuals for a software company in Dallas. Visit Jana at her website, www.janadeleon.com.

Books by Jana DeLeon

HARLEQUIN INTRIGUE
1265—THE SECRET OF CYPRIERE BAYOU
1291—BAYOU BODYGUARD
1331—THE LOST GIRLS OF JOHNSON'S BAYOU

CAST OF CHARACTERS

Ginny Bergeron—No one knew who she was or where she came from, including Ginny. But she made her home in Johnson's Bayou and tried not to think about her mysterious past. Then Paul Stanton showed up, looking for answers.

Paul Stanton—He was separated from his sister by the foster care system seventeen years ago and is determined to find out what happened to her. His answers may lie in Ginny's flickering memories, but his growing attraction to his potential witness isn't sitting well with the P.I.

Madelaine Bergeron—She adopted Ginny after the fire and raised her in Johnson's Bayou. She made a normal life for Ginny, but is afraid the past has come back to haunt her.

Josephine Foster—Everyone sees the tiny, silver-haired woman and assumes she's harmless, but Josephine knows more about the secret lives of Johnson's Bayou residents than the sheriff.

Saul Pritchard—He was the caretaker at the LeBlanc School, but were his pursuits limited to repairing only the home?

Thomas Morgan—He was the contractor in charge of the construction of the LeBlanc School, with a shady past and a lot of unexplained cash.

Mayor Joe Daigle—Johnson's Bayou's mayor would do anything to keep the sixteen-year-old horror from resurfacing in his town.

Sheriff Thomas Blackwell—He was the chief investigator for the fire at the LeBlanc School, but did he know more than what was reflected in the police reports?

Chapter One

Ginny Bergeron stood in front of the café's plate-glass window and stared into the swamp. The setting sun cast an orange glow on the cobblestone street in front of the café and the thick range of cypress trees that littered the swamp beyond the edge of the small town. It was the same view she'd had every day for sixteen years, yet today, it felt different. As if something wasn't right.

"You gonna finish cleaning that coffeepot or just stare out the window all day?"

The booming voice of the heavyset woman behind her made Ginny jump, and she spun around to face Madelaine, the woman who was, for all practical purposes, her mother.

"Sorry," Ginny said. "I guess I wandered there for a minute."

Madelaine gave her an understanding smile and glanced out the window. "It's a beautiful sunset. I finished up in the back, so as soon as those coffeepots are washed, we can leave." She grabbed one of the pots off the warmer behind the counter. "Since you're up here lollygagging, I'll help."

Ginny smiled at Madelaine's teasing, more because

she knew her mother expected it than because she felt like smiling. The beautiful sunset wasn't what had caught Ginny's attention. In fact, Ginny couldn't put her finger on exactly why she'd been staring out the window, or what she expected to see. But she could feel it—something out there didn't belong.

Ginny grabbed the half-empty coffeepot off the table where she'd placed it a couple of minutes earlier and headed behind the counter. Madelaine already had hot water running in the huge stainless steel sink, so Ginny poured out the old coffee and stuck the pot under the stream of water. Some of the steamy water splashed onto her bare hands and she flinched. Her mother glanced over at her bare hands and shook her head, her expression one of long-standing exasperation worn by parents who'd told a child something over and over again in vain.

"I have a pot roast in my Crock-Pot," Madelaine said. "Why don't you come over for dinner and a movie?"

"Great minds think alike. I put a roast in my Crock-Pot this morning."

Madelaine wiped the coffeepot with a clean rag and set it on the counter. "Well, if you're sure."

"I'm sure," Ginny said and placed her clean coffeepot on the counter next to her mother's.

"I guess we'll both be eating pot roast for a week then." Madelaine stared at her for a moment, the uncertainty clear on her face, but finally, being a parent won out. "I worry about you spending so much time alone. You sure you're all right? You've seemed on edge lately."

"I'm fine, and I'm perfectly happy alone. I have

a good library of books." She smiled. "You ought to know, since you gave me most of them."

Madelaine didn't look convinced. "A book isn't the same as having someone else around. Like a man. Then maybe I wouldn't worry as much."

"Really? I haven't noticed that being a problem for you. In fact, in my years with you, I've never known you to even date."

Madelaine waved a hand in dismissal. "That's not the point. I made my choices long ago, and I'm happy with them. I had my run at that hill in my earlier years. Enough to know it wasn't for me. But you haven't so much as taken a step toward it."

Ginny shook her head. "You know good and well that the only single men in Johnson's Bayou are under ten or over sixty. Which would you prefer I take up with?"

"Ain't no one saying you got to remain here the rest of your life. That university in New Orleans wanted to give you a scholarship before. I bet you could get one again."

"And do what?"

"Leave. Leave all this behind and start a new life. A good life."

Ginny placed a hand on Madelaine's arm. "I have a good life. Maybe someday I'll want something different, something else, but for now, this is what's right for me."

Madelaine sighed and kissed Ginny's forehead. "All right then. I'll see you tomorrow morning. Ought to be a busy one with everyone in town preparing for the Fall Festival."

Ginny nodded then followed Madelaine to the front

door of the café and locked it behind her. Ginny gave the café a final glance to make sure everything was in order, then hurried up the staircase at the back of the café kitchen to her apartment.

The apartment consisted of a small living area, an even smaller bedroom and a tiny kitchenette and bathroom. Madelaine had provided her with a worn couch that Ginny had recovered in coarse fabric with light blue and white stripes. An old nineteen-inch television sat across from the couch on a stand with peeling paint that Ginny had bought at a garage sale but hadn't had time to refinish.

She'd taken her bedroom set with her when she'd moved out of her mother's house, and the bed, dresser and nightstand left only a small walking area in the narrow bedroom. The kitchen had room in the corner for a tiny table and two chairs, but nothing else. Some people probably wouldn't consider it much, but for Ginny, it was perfect.

What some would see as sparse, Ginny saw as uncomplicated.

Her life in Johnson's Bayou certainly hadn't started out that way, but Ginny had been determined to make it that way. She'd always found comfort in knowing that today was the same as yesterday and would be the same as tomorrow. But lately, complicated thoughts had roamed her mind, unbidden. Despite her attempts to ignore them or change her mode of thinking, the thoughts kept popping back up, unwanted and uncomfortable.

She laid her keys on the breakfast table and opened the blinds on the window behind the table. The sun had almost disappeared behind the swamp, but she could still see the roofline of the old mansion just above the top of the cypress trees. The LeBlanc School for Girls. Or at least it had been.

What had happened there sixteen years ago? And had she been a part of it? Is that why the house seemed to call to her in the night? All these years, she'd had no inkling of her past, as if her mind had been scrubbed clean of the first six years of her life. She had no answers to the bizarre questions that surrounded her arrival in Johnson's Bayou, despite a significant amount of effort by the local police into searching for those answers.

Ginny had never searched for answers.

Sometimes she thought it was because she was afraid of what she'd find. Other days, she thought it was because nothing she found would change who she was today, and that's all that mattered. Curiosity had never compelled Ginny to visit the LeBlanc School. The police said the fire had completely destroyed the room the resident records were housed in, so no answers were contained there now, even if they had been before.

But lately, she felt anxious…drawn to this window where she could see the top of the house, tucked away in the bayou. Drawn to seek answers to questions she'd never asked out loud. It was as if a giant weight was pressing on her, but for no particular reason that she could determine. Why now, after all these years?

She reached for a shipping box on her table and opened it up. She'd told Madelaine it was supplies for her beadwork. With the festival coming up, Madelaine hadn't even blinked at her explanation of the heavy box. Ginny's jewelry had become quite popular in

Johnson's Bayou, and she'd even had sales to some New Orleans shops. But the item that lay inside wasn't the beads or wire or tools she'd claimed.

She pulled the spotlight out of the box and glanced once more at the woods that lay just beyond her apartment. Every night for a week, she'd taken the spotlight out of the box, determined to walk into the woods, even if only a couple of feet. Determined to prove that nothing was there. That her overactive imagination was playing tricks on her. And every night, she'd placed the spotlight back in the box, closed the blinds and drawn the curtains, trying to eliminate the feeling that she was being watched.

But tonight was going to be different.

She still wore her jeans and T-shirt with the café logo but didn't bother changing. In the time it took to change clothes, she could come up with a million different reasons to delay her trip another night. Before she could change her mind, she hurried out of the apartment and slipped out the back door of the café.

She stood at the edge of the swamp, her strength wavering as she studied the wall of cypress trees and the dense growth beneath them. Dusk had settled over the town behind her, and not even a dim ray of light shone in the swamp.

That's why you have the spotlight.

She took one step into the swamp and studied the brush in front of her, looking for any sign of a path. This was foolish. She should abandon this folly and come back in the daylight.

But in the daylight someone might see…and question.

It had taken years for the whispering about her to

stop. Years for the residents of Johnson's Bayou to feel comfortable in the same room as her. The last thing she wanted to do was spook a group of already superstitious people by fueling their original fears about her—about what she was.

The brush was less dense to the right, and when she directed her spotlight that way she could make out an open area about twenty feet away. She pointed her spotlight toward the clearing and stepped deeper into the swamp. The brush closed in around her, eliminating what was left of the natural light. The sharp branches scratched her bare arms, but she pushed forward until she reached the clearing.

It was small, maybe five feet square, and someone had taken the time to remove all the brush from the area. The ground was solid, dark dirt beneath her feet, not a sign of grass or weeds in sight. Kids, maybe? Although she couldn't imagine kids wanting to play in this area of the swamp, nor their parents allowing it. On the backside of the clearing, a tiny path stretched into the dense brush. Ginny directed her spotlight to the path and pushed through the brush for several minutes until she reached another clearing.

This one was bigger than the last and circular, with charred wood in the center. Ginny frowned. Surely no one was camping out here. Even if one didn't believe the old tales about spooks and haunts, the swamp was filled with plenty of dangers, many of them deadly. Those who'd lived near the swamp their entire lives still preferred to spend the night hours surrounded by four walls.

She studied the wood for a moment and realized it was completely rotted. A piece of it broke off easily in her hand. It had been a long time since someone placed it there and burned it, but that still didn't explain why the brush had not taken the clearing back over. Why the dirt stood barren.

Her spine stiffened suddenly and she stood motionless in the clearing. Her hair stood up on the back of her neck, but she had no idea what had set her off. She listened for the sounds of a night creature on the prowl, but it was almost as if the swamp had gone silent. There wasn't a breath of air, and even the bugs had stopped making noise. She could hear her heart beating in her chest and the sound of her breath as she raggedly drew it in and out.

Then the sound of a child's scream ripped through the night air.

Terror washed over Ginny like rain and held her captive, unable to move. The overwhelming desire to run as fast as she could back to the café was overshadowed by guilt, knowing she needed to help whoever had screamed. She took a deep breath to steady herself and tried to determine which direction the scream had come from. Instinct told her it had been deeper in the swamp and to her right, but she couldn't be sure.

Saying a silent prayer, she slipped into the brush at the far end of the circle and forged ahead. Several minutes later, she stepped out of the swamp and onto the estate grounds of the LeBlanc School. She drew up short and sucked in a breath as the house rose out of the swamp before her. All these years, as she'd studied the roofline from her kitchen window, she'd tried to convince herself that it was just a house. A thing made of stone and wood.

As she looked up at the dark stained-glass windows

that seemed to stare back at her, she knew she'd been wrong. Something malevolent called this place home. Something that remained, even when everyone else had passed from its doors years ago.

A wave of nausea came over her and she took in a deep breath and blew it slowly out. The child. She had to focus on finding the child, and not even let her mind wander to what was happening to the child in this evil place. She took one hesitant step toward the house when someone grabbed her from behind. His arm encircled her neck, almost strangling her, and the rough skin of his palm pressed over her mouth, blocking her scream.

"Don't make a sound," he whispered.

Chapter Two

Ginny was overwhelmed with panic and her knees began to buckle. This was it. She was going to die. Her fear of the swamp had become a self-fulfilling prophecy. Then her captor loosened his grip and spun her around to face him.

He was young, with rugged features and a hard body that she knew was meant for action. The butt of a pistol peeked out of the top of his jeans, but he didn't reach for it. Instead he stared, his eyes assessing every square inch of her.

"Who are you?" he asked.

She stared for a moment, unable to find her voice. "Gi...Ginny Bergeron. I live here." Did he need to know her name if he was going to kill her?

He raised one eyebrow and stared at her a moment. "You live here—in this abandoned house?"

"No. I mean, I live in Johnson's Bayou."

"Do you always trespass on private property, Ms. Bergeron?"

Some of Ginny's fear began to dissipate and was quickly replaced with agitation. Apparently, her attacker was interested only in harassing her, not hurting her, or he could have been done a long time ago. "The entire swamp is not private property, and I didn't realize I was running toward the house. I was trying to help the child."

His eyes narrowed. "What child?"

"I heard a scream. Right after I entered the swamp. It sounded like a child."

"You're sure? There are plenty of creatures out in this swamp that make noise. Maybe it was one of them that you heard?"

Ginny bristled. "Look, I've lived next to this swamp my entire life. I know what animals sound like, and none of them sound like a child screaming bloody murder. Why are you harassing me?"

The man pulled the gun from his waistband, and she took a step back.

"What direction did the scream come from?" he asked.

Ginny stared at the gun for a second before answering. "I thought it came from here. I mean, I came in the direction of the scream and ended up at the house."

He nodded. "Do you know how to get back to town?"

"Yes. It's due east. I have a great sense of direction."

He didn't look convinced. "You need to go home. Lock your doors and forget you ever saw me out here. Is that clear?"

"Crystal." The reply had barely left her lips before he rushed off toward the front of the house.

Ginny watched his retreating back for a second then spun around and ran through the brush toward town. She didn't stop running until she was upstairs in her apartment, with the doors closed, locked and dead-bolted and every blind and curtain in the apartment closed tight.

PAUL STANTON GRIPPED his pistol in one hand and shone his flashlight around the cavernous entryway of the old house. He strained to make out a sound, any indication there was life in the dilapidated structure, but all he heard was the night air whistling through the broken stained-glass window at the top of the vaulted ceiling.

Unbelievable! What in the world was she doing roaming around the swamp without a weapon? The blond-haired waif didn't appear skilled enough to take on a box of kittens, much less any of the creatures she might run into in the swamp. Clearly, she was nuts. Sane people didn't stroll through a swamp at night with nothing but a hundred-dollar spotlight. Which left him wondering whether or not she'd really heard a scream.

With all the tales surrounding the house, he was surprised someone from town would even venture to this area of the swamp, especially after dark. In fact, he'd been counting on that fear to keep from being caught himself. Perhaps curiosity had gotten the better of her, because she didn't seem overly confident about being there. What bothered him more than anything was that a single woman with no weapon felt compelled to wander around these woods at night. She must have a darned good reason, and he couldn't help but wonder what it was.

He took a cursory look at the areas of the home that were easily passable, but there weren't many. The fire had destroyed a large section of the home, supposedly where the records on the girls had been held, but even the areas that hadn't been touched by fire had obviously had visitors. All the cabinets in the kitchen were open, the drawers pulled completely out from the frames. Furniture had been upended so that not a single piece was left upright.

Shards of fabric hung from upholstered furniture, and piles of stuffing, covered with mold and dirt long ago, rested everywhere. Time alone would have destroyed the fabric, but it couldn't have removed all the stuffing into neat piles. More likely, someone had slit the fabric and searched through the furniture after the fire. What were they looking for? Money? Jewels?

Or were they like him—looking for answers?

He couldn't picture the spotlight waif tearing through furniture with a hunting knife, but maybe she was a good actress and had fooled him completely. Maybe she hadn't been afraid or startled in the least and the story about the child had been designed to distract him from whatever she was doing at the house. The worst part was, it had worked.

He walked down a long hallway and shone his light into the rooms, looking for any sign of recent entry, but he found only the same mess as he'd seen in the front room. No little girl. No intruder. No bogeyman.

At the end of the hall, he looked out a huge picture window into the pitch-black swamp and blew out a breath. He had intended to make it to the house from the backside of the swamp during daylight. It would have been far easier to search, and no one lived anywhere near the back entrance into the swamp he'd planned to use. But work had delayed him and he'd arrived at sunset. Not willing to wait to get a first glance, he'd foolishly made the choice to approach the house entering the swamp in town, as the town was closer to the house than the back way he'd originally chosen. Now, he'd been caught by a local.

Tomorrow morning, he needed to find out what he could about the woman, Ginny Bergeron. Make sure she wasn't going to be a problem. Because another problem was the last thing he needed.

GINNY PULLED HER LONG, straight hair through a pony-tail holder and smoothed out the wrinkles in her café T-shirt. She'd overslept, which was rare, but then she usually didn't spend part of her night scared out of her wits by a stranger in the swamp and then sit up for hours with every light in her apartment blazing. She'd even overcooked the roast and now had tough, leathery sandwiches to look forward to for days.

Her mind had raced last night, even after she'd finally drifted off to sleep, and plagued her with dreams so vivid that she felt she was there. The house and a child were in her dreams, but she couldn't see the child's face. Now, in the bright light of the bathroom mirror, she wondered if the child in her dreams had been her. In the bright light of the bathroom mirror, she almost wondered if she'd heard the scream.

She shook her head. No, she wasn't crazy. The scream had been real, but many things had stopped her from picking up the phone last night and calling the police. No proof. Everyone in town looking at her strangely again. The list went on and on, and there was no time to cover it all now.

She locked the apartment door behind her and hurried down the stairs. Today was the first day of the town's annual Fall Festival and the café would be crowded early so that everyone could get to the town square and set up their booths. If a little girl was missing, Ginny would be certain to hear about it during breakfast service. Then she'd go to the police. If no one was missing, she would have to admit that her imagination had played tricks on her and figure out how she felt about that.

In the meantime, she was almost late for work, and the last thing she needed was to give her mother any indication that her life was not calm and, if not perfect, at least boring. Madelaine looked up from her bowl of pancake mix as Ginny exited the stairwell into the kitchen. She gave her a critical once-over, then went back to mixing the batter.

"Thought maybe you were calling in sick," Madelaine said.

"No, sorry. Just overslept. I stayed up too late working on jewelry," Ginny lied.

The bit of worry in Madelaine's face relaxed. Her mother knew better than anyone how time could escape Ginny when she was making jewelry. "I thought you had everything ready for the festival already?"

"I did…do…just a last-minute thought." Ginny tied an apron around her waist and slipped an order pad into one of the front pockets. She glanced down at her watch. "Is the coffee on out front?"

Madelaine nodded. "Did it first thing. Turned on the two pots in here, as well. Gonna be busy this morning."

"Praise God and bring the customers," Ginny said, quoting one of Madelaine's favorite sayings.

Madelaine grinned. "If business goes well this

week, we might even close for a bit. Go up to New Orleans and have somebody paint our toenails pink."

Ginny laughed, a feeling of normalcy returning to her in a rush. "That sounds wonderful." She glanced at the front of the café, where a crowd was already gathering outside. "It's a couple minutes till, but I think I'll take pity and let them in."

Madelaine nodded and Ginny opened the front door of the café at 5:49 a.m. to a happy roar of locals.

Two hours later, the last of the townspeople had completed the breakfast rush and Ginny slumped in a chair in the kitchen. Madelaine handed her a glass of iced tea and took a seat on a stool in front of the giant double sink teaming full of dishes.

"Busy one," Madelaine said as Ginny took a huge drink of the cold tea.

"I think the good weather's bringing everyone out."

Madelaine nodded. "Should be a good turnout for the festival. Maybe some more New Orleans stores will see your jewelry and want to stock it."

"I've got my fingers crossed. It's doing well at Sarah's shop, but I'd love to have more distribution."

Madelaine opened her mouth to reply, but the dinging of the bell on the front door stopped her. She motioned to Ginny, who was already rising from her chair. "You take a break for a minute. I'll get the order. You can deliver the food."

Ginny sank back down, grateful for the reprieve, no matter how slight. A couple of minutes later, Madelaine hustled back into the kitchen, scooped a huge cinnamon roll onto a plate and handed it to Ginny.

"That's it?"

"No. He wants an omelet but asked to have this out

first. And he'll likely need a coffee refill, the way he was downing the first cup."

"Who is it?" Ginny asked as she started toward the kitchen door.

Madelaine shrugged as she cracked eggs on the skillet. "Probably here for the festival."

This early? The thought flashed through Ginny's mind and just as quickly, a second thought hit her and she sucked in a breath. Surely not.

She pushed open the kitchen door just enough to scan the café without being seen. It was empty except for one booth on the far end from the door occupied by the man who, unfortunately, had his back to Ginny. *You're being foolish. What are the odds?*

She pushed the door completely open and stepped into the café. She was only a couple of feet from the man's table when he turned slightly to look up at her.

It was him. The man from the swamp.

Her heart rate spiked and she dropped her gaze to her hands, clutching the plate so hard, she thought it would snap. It took every ounce of control for her to set the plate in front of him. She forced herself to raise her head and meet his gaze, and she was surprised to notice he seemed out of sorts as well. He was older than she'd originally thought, maybe early thirties, but then her eyes had been on his gun last night and not him. His dark brown hair was a little long and lay in natural waves. Green eyes studied her as she reached for the coffeepot on the counter station and refilled his empty cup.

"Your omelet will be ready in a couple of minutes," she said, trying to keep her voice even. "Is there anything else I can get you?"

He shook his head, but Ginny got the impression there was something he wanted to say but didn't. She took that as her cue to exit, but as she turned to walk away, he grabbed her arm. She looked down at his hand, wrapped around her wrist, and wondered why this man made her feel so nervous, so off-balance.

"I probably owe you an apology," he said and drew his hand back from her arm. "I didn't mean to scare you last night, but you surprised me. I didn't expect to find anyone out in the swamp at that time of night."

"Neither did I."

He gave her an uneasy chuckle. "Yeah, I guess not. So anyway, sorry I grabbed you."

"It's okay." Ginny was more than ready to end the uncomfortable conversation, but she took a breath then blurted out, "Did you find the child?"

He stared at her for a moment, the indecision in his eyes apparent. Finally, he shook his head. "No. I looked around, but I didn't see any trace that someone else had been near the house, and I didn't hear anything."

She bit her lower lip, knowing she should just return to the kitchen and forget she'd ever been traipsing around the swamp. "Nothing at all?"

"I'm sorry," he said and gave her a sympathetic look.

She gave him a brief nod and walked back toward the kitchen. *Great, now he thinks I'm crazy and feels sorry for me.*

Hell, who was she kidding? Despite her certainty last night, maybe she was crazy. There hadn't been so much as a whisper about a missing child in the café all morning, and that kind of story would have been huge news in Johnson's Bayou. Maybe she'd imagined the scream. That's what she got for letting something build for so long without addressing it. She should have stalked straight to that house the first time her mind latched on it. Instead, she'd put it off for so long that her imagination had run wild.

Before she slipped into the kitchen, she glanced back at the man. She noticed he hadn't bothered to explain what he'd been doing in the swamp at night, and she hadn't wanted to ask. But she wondered. Now, he sat at an angle in the booth, talking on his cell phone, and from the look on his face, he didn't like what he'd just heard.

Chapter Three

Paul gripped the phone, anxious for the information Mike, his partner at their New Orleans detective agency, was about to provide. "You've found something?"

"I may have a line on something, but I can't be positive. The information on that case is so sketchy."

"You thinking cover-up?"

"Not necessarily. It may have just been a case of inexperienced cops with a situation far beyond what they were qualified to handle. The whole thing is pretty weird. I mean, all those kids dying but no one coming to claim them. It reeks all the way around, Paul."

"Yeah, I know, but it's an avenue I have to check. So what did you find?"

"One student survived, for sure, but the bodies of one other student and the headmistress were never recovered. Then this is where it gets weird. The day after the fire, a girl walked out of the swamp and into town, but no one could identify her as a student. No one in the town, even the locals who worked at the home, had ever laid eyes on her."

"Well, who did she say she was?"

"She didn't know. Total amnesia."

"Great. The best witness I might have and she doesn't remember anything. Any idea where the girls are now?"

"I tracked the girl rescued from the house as far as a hospital in New Orleans, but the trail went cold after that. You'll probably have to speak to people off the record. The hospital's not likely to give you anything without a court order."

Paul blew out a breath, knowing his partner was right, and that as things stood right now, he had no legal grounds to gain such a document. "And the other? The mystery girl?"

"That one's a little trickier. There's nothing in the police records. No follow-up at all, so the best I can do is a rumor from an old aunt of mine that lives down that way. She heard that the girl was adopted by someone in town. Thinks the woman who adopted her might own a restaurant or something."

Paul clutched the phone and shot a glance toward the kitchen. Could it possibly be the café waif was looking for answers in the swamp, as well? "You're sure?"

"No, I'm not sure about any of it, but my aunt is certain that's what she heard. It may be something. It may not."

"Okay, thanks. I'll check out a few things here today and be in touch tonight." Paul set the cell phone on the table and looked out the glass front of the café into the swamp. Ginny couldn't be the child he was searching for. She was the right age, but the child he sought had brown eyes, something she'd always complained about. Ginny's eyes were bright blue.

But if Ginny was the child who had wandered out of

the swamp, maybe she remembered something. After all these years, surely some memory, even if seemingly insignificant, had returned. She was the only potential witness to a horrible crime, if you believed the rumors that the fire had been set. That might explain why she was out in the swamp after dark. Maybe her memory was returning.

"Here you go." The older woman who'd taken his order slid a plate with an omelet and toast on the table in front of him. Paul looked up, momentarily disappointed that Ginny wasn't delivering his food, but then, he could hardly force her to sit in the booth and tell all her secrets. She'd seemed nervous when he apologized earlier, and the last thing he wanted to do was alienate himself from the one lead he had. What he needed to do was find out more about Ginny, and then maybe he'd be able to design an approach.

"It looks great," he said and glanced around the café. "Is it always so quiet in here?"

"Oh, no, not usually. But most of the locals have booths at the festival, so they've already been in and out. Is that what you're here for?"

"Yes," Paul lied, figuring the festival would make a good cover, at least for a couple of days. "I'd heard a bit about it and thought I'd check it out. Maybe get in some fishing afterward. I just didn't realize it started this early."

"The official kickoff is at noon, but setup takes a while for those with a lot of merchandise. I just sent my daughter off to set up her booth. I'll likely close everything up once you're done and head to the festival myself to help people out."

"That sounds great. What does your daughter sell?"

"Handcrafted jewelry. She even fashions some of her own metal," she said, her voice full of pride. "A store in New Orleans is selling some pieces already."

Paul smiled. "My aunt has a boutique in Baton Rouge. I'll take some pictures and maybe buy a few samples of your daughter's work. She loves featuring items by Louisiana designers."

The woman beamed. "That would be fantastic. Well, my name's Madelaine, and my daughter's Ginny. I'm gonna get out of here and let you finish your breakfast."

She hustled back to the kitchen, and Paul turned his attention to the omelet. The festival was the perfect cover, and it provided an excellent reason for him to ask some questions about Ginny, both to Ginny and to others.

Less than one day in town and he already had a lead. Not bad at all.

THE MAN WATCHED HER from across the town square as she unpacked jewelry from cardboard boxes and arranged it on a folding table covered with black velvet draping. She didn't appear different from what she did any other day, but he knew something was different. He'd noticed her staring out the window of the café lately, looking toward the abandoned school.

After all these years, she'd never seemed to care. Never wanted to talk about her past when people, even specialists like doctors and counselors, tried to bring it up. So why did it seem her curiosity was developing now? What had changed? Nothing in town or within her immediate family and friends. He was sure about that, as he knew everyone in Johnson's Bayou.

Was she starting to remember?

He hoped not, because he liked Ginny. Liked the young woman she'd become. It would be a shame to have to kill her now.

GINNY TOOK THE CASH from another happy customer and handed her a bag of jewelry in exchange. The woman thanked her and hurried off to meet her husband, who'd waited almost patiently for the thirty minutes the woman had taken to pick out the perfect pair of earrings. Ginny tucked the cash into her apron and smiled at Mrs. Foster, who was giving her a thumbs-up from her table of baked goods across the brick walkway.

With her table empty of customers for the first time that day, Ginny decided to walk across to Mrs. Foster's table and grab up something good before it was all gone. Mrs. Foster's baking was famous in Johnson's Bayou, and Ginny didn't want to miss out.

"You been doing some good business today," the silver-haired Mrs. Foster said as Ginny approached. "You might sell out before me."

Ginny laughed. "That will be the day." Ginny scanned the table of picked-over goodies. "No more coffee cake?" she asked, trying not to let her disappointment show in her voice.

Mrs. Foster reached beneath the table and brought up a coffee cake, a big grin on her face. "I saved one for you."

"Bless you," Ginny said and pulled some money out of her apron.

Mrs. Foster shook her head. "Your money's no good

here. Those earrings you made me are still the most coveted at bingo night."

Ginny smiled. "Then we're even, because I might have a matching necklace tucked under my table for you."

Mrs. Foster's face lit up and she clapped her hands. "That old biddy Adelaide will never get over it. You've made my day, Ginny."

Mrs. Foster's gaze shifted past Ginny and she pointed. "Got a new customer. Nice-looking one, too."

Ginny looked back at her table, then froze. It was him.

She supposed Mrs. Foster was right. He *was* good-looking, when she could manage to separate the man standing at her booth from the man who'd scared her half to death the night before. He studied the jewelry with more interest than she would have expected from a guy, but she immediately chided herself for such a sexist thought. For all she knew, he may have a wife or girlfriend at home whom he was purchasing for. She knew she should go back to her table, but she hesitated. He made her uneasy in a way she'd never felt before.

Finally, she took a deep breath and began to cross the walkway. Suddenly, he stiffened, then reached for a custom metal necklace at the end of her table. He stared at the piece, his expression a mixture of surprise and confusion.

"Can I help you?" she asked.

He whirled around to face her and shoved the necklace at her. "Where did you get this design?"

Surprised by his obvious agitation, she took a step back. "I...I didn't get it anywhere."

He waved one hand at her table, his frustration apparent. "You used it in half of your jewelry. Why? What does it mean to you?"

Ginny stared, not certain what answer he was looking for, but clearly she didn't have the right one. "It doesn't mean anything to me. It's just a design I thought of. It was popular with the customers, so I adopted it as a sort of signature."

He narrowed his eyes at her. "You just thought of the design? Just like that?"

Ginny bristled, done with his attitude. "Yes, that's what artists do. They just think of things then create them. If you're not interested in purchasing that necklace, please return it to the table and be on your way, Mr...." She trailed off, realizing that he'd never given her his name.

"Stanton. Paul Stanton."

He studied her face with an intensity that was almost alarming. Ginny got the distinct impression he was trying to decide if she was lying, although about what she had absolutely no idea.

"I'll take this necklace," he said and pulled out his wallet. "How much?"

Ginny's initial instinct was to refuse to sell him the necklace and demand that Paul Stanton leave her table, but she was afraid he wouldn't be put off that easily. More than anything, she wanted this angry, suspicious man out of her personal space. "Twenty dollars."

He pulled a twenty out of his wallet and handed it to her. "You're certain you've never seen this design somewhere before?"

"What do you want me to say—that I stole the design from someone? Well, I didn't. I had that image in my mind years before I began designing jewelry."

Since the day I walked out of the swamp and into John-son's Bayou.

"How long?"

Ginny frowned. "How long have I been designing jewelry?"

"No. How long have you had that image in your mind?"

"I don't see—"

"Just tell me."

His voice had a desperate edge to it, and Ginny began to see something behind the frustration in his expression. Fear?

"Sixteen years," Ginny replied. *As long as I can re-member.*

He stared at the swirl of metal that lay on his palm. "Sixteen years," he whispered and clutched his hand around the necklace before he turned and walked away.

What in the world? Ginny stared at his retreating figure, at a complete loss over their exchange. She didn't think the design was stolen. Surely, she'd have seen it before now if that was the case, but Paul Stanton had acted as if he'd seen the pattern before. Seeing the design on her jewelry had clearly bothered him.

But why?

She watched as he disappeared into the festival crowd, somehow knowing she hadn't seen the last of him. Turning to her table, she looked at the rows of metal pieces, many fashioned in the same swirl of circles with one circle in the middle, giving the design a flower-like appearance. She'd never questioned where the design had come from. It had always been there.

Even though it was at least eighty degrees outside, she felt a chill run over her. Was the design part of her past? The single item she'd brought out of the woods with her?

And if so, what did it mean to Paul Stanton?

Chapter Four

Ginny placed what remained of her jewelry in the plastic storage container and strapped it on the dolly she'd borrowed from the café. It had been a good day for sales, and despite her somewhat unnerving run-in with Paul Stanton, she felt upbeat as she pulled her purse strap over her shoulder.

"Need any help?" Madelaine's voice sounded behind her, and she turned to smile at her mother, who was laden down with bags.

"Looks like I should be asking you that question." She pulled the top off her storage container and collected some of her mother's shopping bags, dropping them inside. Her mother unwound more bags from her other arm and continued adding to the container until it was full. She was still clutching two more bags.

"Whew, that's a relief," Madelaine said, rubbing her forearm with her free hand.

Ginny secured the top on the container, shaking her head. "What in the world did you buy? You live here year-round with everyone selling their wares. You don't have to buy everything at one time."

"Carol's aunt was here—the one I told you about, remember?"

"The seamstress?"

"That's the one. When we chatted at Carol and Glenn's anniversary party, I mentioned wanting new tablecloths and such for the café but not being able to find what I was looking for premade. I was going to call her to get some pricing, but one thing led to another, and well, you know how it is."

Ginny swung the dolly around behind her and they started walking down Main Street toward the café. "You forgot."

"Exactly."

"So what's with all the packages?"

"The aunt had an idea for the café based on what I'd described and made up some tablecloths and napkins, figuring if I wasn't interested, she'd sell them at her shop in New Orleans."

Madelaine dug in one of her bags and pulled out a napkin fashioned from patches of bright patterned materials in turquoise, pink, green and yellow. She handed the napkin to Ginny. "How perfect is that?"

Ginny looked down at the splash of colorful fabrics and smiled. "It is perfect and totally you." She handed the napkin back to Madelaine. "What about valances? That blue gingham with the sunflowers has been hanging there since I was a little girl."

"She's coming by tomorrow to measure the windows. I'm also thinking it's time for a fresh coat of paint, maybe a sunny yellow to match that color in the napkins. What do you think?"

"I think it sounds like a lot of work…but nice."

Madelaine waved a hand in dismissal. "I'll hire Saul Pritchard to do the painting. He finished up Carol's bedroom last week, so I know he's got the time. So

I guess the almost-empty container means you had a good day."

"It was an excellent day. I sold everything but ten pieces, and a couple of buyers for bigger shops bought pieces and took pictures and business cards."

"Whoo! I'm telling you, one day you're going to be famous and you're going to buy me a nice beach house in the Bahamas, with one of those cute guys who bring you fancy drinks."

"A cabana boy?" Ginny laughed. "If I get rich and famous, it's a deal."

"Carol said she saw a likely candidate at your booth today when she passed with her grandkids. From her description, I thought it might be that good-looking young man who was in the café this morning."

Ginny nodded, struggling not to frown. "He bought a necklace."

"That's it?" The disappointment in Madelaine's voice was clear.

"Yes, that's it. What was he supposed to do?"

"Well, he said he had family that owned a store, but maybe he plans on taking the piece to them to see. And I thought…well…oh, never mind."

"You thought since he was over ten and under sixty, I should jump him at the festival?"

"Of course not, but a nice lunch wouldn't be out of line. Oh well, he said he was taking a bit of a vacation. Maybe you'll see him again before the festival is over."

Ginny stopped in front of the café and pulled her keys from her purse to unlock the front door, trying not to think about what Madelaine had said. She'd bet everything she owned that Paul Stanton was not on vacation. He had far too much intensity for a man who was supposed to be relaxing. Ginny was certain he was in Johnson's Bayou for a reason, but she didn't even want to know what it was. She just wanted him to leave her alone.

"You coming in?" Ginny asked.

"No. I'm pooped. I'm gonna take a long shower and go to bed early." She gave Ginny a kiss on the cheek. "Just leave my bags in the kitchen. I'll deal with them tomorrow."

Ginny pulled the dolly into the kitchen and unloaded her mother's bags on the desk in the back corner of the kitchen. She grabbed the almost-empty container and hauled it upstairs with her to refill for tomorrow's display. She balanced the wide container on her hip and the wall to unlock her apartment, but the instant she stepped inside, she knew something was wrong.

She stood stock-still just inside the front door and felt the hair on the back of her neck rise. She listened for sounds that would indicate anyone was there, but all she heard was the quiet ticking of the kitchen clock. Scanning every square inch of the room, she tried to find something out of place. Something that would explain her fear, but everything appeared as it had when she'd left that morning.

She started to move, but then a scent wafted past her nose. The faint smell of musk, like a man's aftershave. Without a sound, she placed the container on the floor next to the door and walked toward her bedroom, leaving the door to the apartment wide open in case she needed to make a run for it. She stopped just outside the bathroom and reached around the wall with her hand to flip on the lights. Light flooded the tiny room,

and one quick look was all it took for her to know it
was empty. The curtain was pulled back on the bath-
tub, just as she'd left it that morning, so no one could
be hiding inside, and the tiny bathroom didn't have a
linen closet.

Easing down the hall, she reached inside her bedroom and turned on the lights. The room appeared un-
disturbed, and she was glad she'd left in a hurry that
morning and left her closet door open. It was so small
that she could see every square inch from the doorway,
and no one lurked inside. Her bed was platform style
with drawers for storage underneath, so no one could
be hiding there.

Relief washed over her and she plopped down on the
bed, chiding herself for scaring herself half to death
over nothing. She needed to get a grip on her overactive imagination. It had been getting worse for some
time, but ever since her trip into the woods and her
run-in with Paul Stanton, it seemed to be in overdrive.
She pulled open the drawer on her nightstand to retrieve lip balm she kept inside and froze.

Her diary had been moved.

She leaned over for a closer look, but she knew it
wasn't where she'd left it. It wasn't off by much, but she
was almost anal about fitting it exactly into the corner
of the drawer. Now, it lay about an inch from the side.
Lifting the journal from the drawer, she inspected the
bookmark. Just as she suspected, it was off. The pink
flower that she always left peeking out from the top
of the journal was buried halfway in the book.

Suddenly, she remembered that she'd left the front
door wide open and she jumped up from the bed, dropping her journal on the bed as she dashed out of the

room. She slammed the door and slid the dead bolt into place, then leaned back against it, trying to slow her racing heart.

No one but Madelaine had a key to her apartment, or the café, for that matter. And she couldn't think of any reason at all that someone would break into her apartment to read her journal. She didn't have much of value, but she kept a stash of cash in the same nightstand as the journal, and it was still there. It didn't make sense. Why would anyone go through the trouble of finding an undetected way into the café and her apartment just to read the ramblings of a waitress?

Paul Stanton!

Ever since he'd grabbed her in the woods last night, he'd shown up everywhere she was. Granted, it was a small town, so that wasn't hard to do, but Ginny didn't believe for a moment that he'd picked Johnson's Bayou at random for a vacation and then went roaming around the woods at night carrying a gun for relaxation.

Then there was that scene at the festival today. She'd seen his expression when he asked her about the necklace. He was surprised and agitated and afraid, all at the same time, just as he had been when he'd found her in the woods that night. But why?

Ginny crossed the room to the kitchenette and pulled a bottle of wine out of the refrigerator. She had moved past scared to angry. A glass of wine and a hot bath were in order. It had been a long day of work between the café and the festival, and she had to do it all again tomorrow.

She took a sip of the wine and stared out the kitchen window into the woods. If Paul Stanton had the nerve to show up at the café or the festival tomorrow, she was going to give him a piece of her mind.

In fact, she was almost looking forward to it.

PAUL TIMED HIS ENTRY into the café just after the locals had cleared out to set up for the festival. He'd barely slept, his mind rolling around every possibility associated with the jewelry he'd purchased from Ginny the day before. The jewelry laid out in the same swirl of circles that his sister used to draw on everything—her signature, she used to call it. Their mother had even helped her paint the design on her bedroom walls in bright pinks and blues.

It wasn't impossible that two people would have the same idea, but it was highly unlikely. And if Ginny was the girl who had wandered out of the woods the day the LeBlanc School had burned, then Lord only knew what might be locked in her memory. If her lost memories contained anything to do with his sister, he intended to figure out a way to access them. Surely, she would understand…would help, if he explained the situation. She'd seemed nice enough, despite his less-than-polite behavior, and her mother had definitely shown all the signs of Southern hospitality.

He slipped into an empty booth at the back of the café, as far away as possible from the few patrons who were still lingering. Until he had a better idea of exactly what had happened at that school all those years ago, it was best to keep his purpose in town hidden from the masses. Plus, if he asked Ginny personal questions and she got uncomfortable, locals would probably jump in to protect her. That was typical small-town behavior.

The couple sitting nearest to his booth rose right after he'd taken his seat and left some money on the table. Perfect timing. Now all he needed was for Ginny to come over with her order pad. He hadn't seen her when he walked in, but she was probably in the back plating food or running dirty dishes through the wash.

The door to the kitchen swung open and he took a deep breath, mentally preparing the words he wanted to say. A second later, he let out the breath in a whoosh of disappointment as Madelaine approached his table, a big smile on her face.

"Morning," she said. "You want coffee?"

"Yes, please," he said, trying not to let his disappointment show.

Madelaine stopped at a pot on the counter to pour him a cup of coffee, then placed it on the table in front of him. "Guess the food didn't kill you yesterday."

"No. In fact, your omelet is one of the best I've ever had."

Madelaine blushed a bit. "Oh, well, what a nice thing to say. Did you enjoy the festival yesterday?"

"Yes. I was impressed with the variety of the artists."

"Ginny said you bought a necklace from her. Do you think your aunt might be interested in carrying some of her stuff?"

Paul's mind went blank for a moment and then he remembered the lie that had rolled off his tongue the day before. "It's certainly possible," he said, suddenly realizing why Madelaine was steering the conversation to Ginny.

Which also gave him the perfect opportunity to inquire about her. "I didn't get a chance to talk with her yesterday," he said. "I was hoping to catch her this morning. Has she already left for the festival?"

Madelaine beamed. "No. She ran upstairs for a second. Just let me take your order so I can get it started and I'll send her right out to chat with you."

"Great," Paul said and ordered the breakfast special.

Madelaine stuffed her pad in her apron and hurried into the kitchen, still smiling. Paul felt a momentary twinge of guilt for deliberately misleading the nice woman, but it passed quickly. A little white lie was a small price to pay if it led him to information about his sister.

A couple of minutes later, Ginny came through the kitchen door and into the café. She looked toward his booth and hesitated just a moment before continuing to make her way over. She did not look happy to see him.

"I don't know who you think you are," she said, glaring down at him, "but I want you to leave here before I call the police."

Paul stared for a moment before launching into action. "Wait," he said as she started to move away. "I'm sorry I offended you yesterday, but being rude isn't an offense you need the police to deal with."

"Breaking into my apartment is."

"I didn't.... Someone broke into your apartment? Look, I swear, it wasn't me. I don't even know where you live."

She studied his face, and he waited for her to draw a conclusion. Surely, the shock he felt was clear in his expression. If not, then he was sunk. It was much harder to prove you hadn't done something than proving you had. She bit her lower lip and rolled an end of her apron between her fingers.

"But you want something from me," she said finally. "And I don't believe for a minute it's my jewelry."

Paul ran one hand through his hair, not wanting to immediately launch into his reasons but knowing he needed to explain enough to keep her from running. "No. I'm not interested in your jewelry—at least, not as a buyer."

"Are you still accusing me of stealing that design?" Ginny's face flushed.

"No. That's not it at all." Paul saw the kitchen door open a crack and Madelaine peeked over at them. "Look, I need to talk to you. It's personal and I don't want anyone else to know what I'm doing here. Is there any way you can take a break?"

Ginny glanced back at the kitchen and Madelaine ducked back inside. "Let me get your breakfast and tell my mom I'm going to speak to you a bit before heading to the festival. We're closing soon, anyway."

Relief coursed through him. "Thank you. I promise I'll explain everything."

"You better," Ginny said, then spun around and headed back into the kitchen.

Paul watched her walk through the door to the kitchen and tried to organize his thoughts. He'd hoped to get information from her without divulging the real reason behind his query, but if someone had broken into her apartment, that changed everything. The timing could be totally coincidental, but it would be one heck of a coincidence.

And one that Paul wasn't ready to buy.

Chapter Five

Ginny hurried back into the kitchen, her emotions all over the place. She didn't believe Paul was the person who'd broken into her apartment. The look of shock on his face was genuine, unless he was the best actor she'd ever met. But he was a man with secrets, and for some reason he seemed to think his secrets involved or included her. That unnerved her on many levels, especially as she'd never met the man before that night in the woods. What could he possibly want with her?

And if Paul Stanton hadn't broken into her apartment, then who had?

She broke off her thoughts as she approached the grill, hoping the stress she felt didn't show on her face. Madelaine turned from the grill with Paul's breakfast order. "I saw you talking to Mr. Cutie." She gave Ginny a big smile. "So is he interested in your jewelry, or something else?"

Ginny forced a smile. "He would like to talk to me some about my designs. I told him I could spare a few minutes while he ate, if that's all right."

"Of course. The café's almost empty, and I've just got to clean this grill and rinse the coffeepots. Take all the time you need. I'm going to finish up in here then head out to the festival. You can lock up the front when you're done."

Ginny took the plate from Madelaine and slipped bottles of catsup and Tabasco in her apron. "Thanks," Ginny said and hurried out of the kitchen with the food before Madelaine could clue in to how nervous she was. The woman could read her far too well for Ginny to fool her for long.

She placed the plate, catsup and Tabasco on the table in front of Paul, refilled his coffee and poured herself a cup before sliding into the booth across from him. The last of the patrons said goodbye as they stepped out of the café, and Ginny gave them a wave. "My mom is going to finish up in the back, but I don't have very long before I have to get to the festival. Please tell me what this is about."

Paul nodded and pulled out his wallet. He flipped it open and showed Ginny a license inside.

Ginny stared at the license in surprise. "A detective? What in the world…I mean, why would a detective need anything from me?"

"I'm looking for a missing child. She'd be a young woman now, but she went missing sixteen years ago."

Ginny's pulse began to race. "And you think I'm her?"

"No. You don't have the right eye color. Her eyes were brown and I think she's probably a little older than you, but not by much."

"I don't understand, Mr. Stanton. There are no other adopted women my age in Johnson's Bayou, and if I'm not the girl you're looking for, then I don't know how I can help."

"I thought the girl I'm looking for may have been at

the school in the woods. You're the girl who wandered out of the swamp the day after the school caught fire, aren't you?"

Ginny froze. Of all the things that had ran through her mind, this wasn't one of them, which was stupid since her first run-in with Paul Stanton had been at the LeBlanc School.

"I…yes, that was me. But I still don't see what good that does you."

"I hoped that you may remember something…anything that would help me find out if she was at the LeBlanc School."

"But I don't remember anything. I never have. I don't even know if *I* was at the LeBlanc School. "

"Then why were you in the woods that night at the house?"

"I don't know."

He narrowed his eyes. "So you normally stroll through a swamp at night, carrying an expensive spotlight?" he asked. "And don't tell me you were hunting. I won't buy it."

"I was, oh, I don't know what I was doing. I guess I thought if I saw the house that maybe…"

Paul stared at her, clearly surprised. "You've never been to the house before that night? That's hard to believe."

"I never had a reason to go. Knowing what happened that night wasn't going to change my life now. I don't expect you to understand."

Paul stirred his coffee, silent. After a couple of seconds, he spoke. "I understand. The truth of what happened that night must be horrid, or your mind wouldn't have blocked it all this time. Remembering won't add any value to your life now, and in fact it may only take away."

Ginny stared. "You surprise me, Mr. Stanton."

"Please call me Paul." He gave her a sad smile. "I know what it's like to live in the past. Part of you moves forward every day, but you're not really existing in this point in time. You're not really living because the part of you clinging to the past weighs you down—steals a part of you so that you can't be whole."

Ginny felt the weight of his sadness, and a thought flashed through her mind. "You knew her—the missing girl?"

"Her name is Kathy. She's my sister."

"Oh, no!" Ginny reached across the table and placed her hand on Paul's. "I'm so sorry. I can't imagine losing someone so close and never knowing what happened. You think she was at the LeBlanc School? But why didn't your parents come claim her after the fire?"

"Our parents were killed in a car accident, and we had no other family. We were separated by the foster care system, and I stopped hearing from her sixteen years ago. When I was old enough to insist on tracking her down, I found out that she'd been 'lost.'"

"How do you lose a child you're being paid to protect?" The thought horrified Ginny.

"I'd love an answer to that, but her foster parents disappeared, as well. Their identities were fakes, and I've never been able to trace them any further."

Ginny's mind raced with all the possibilities of what could have happened to his sister, and none of them were good. "What made you think your sister might have been at the LeBlanc School?"

"I didn't really, before I came here. Any more than I thought I would find her when I looked into a hundred other cases of dead girls who'd never been identified, but then I saw your jewelry…"

Ginny gasped. "The design?"

Paul nodded. "My sister used to draw that design all the time. It was on every school notebook…my mom even helped her paint it on her bedroom wall."

"You think I saw that design at the LeBlanc School—that your sister drew it somewhere and it stuck in my mind." Ginny took a deep breath then blew it slowly out. "I wish I could help you, but I swear I don't remember anything, not even the design. It's just always been in my mind."

"But yet, you went into the woods at night. If you really don't remember and don't care to, why did you go?"

Ginny lowered her gaze to the tabletop. "You'd think it was crazy," she said, almost angry with herself that she cared what he thought. She barely knew him. Why should his opinion of her matter?

This time Paul reached across the table to squeeze her hand. "I would never think you're crazy. Please, talk to me."

"I feel something. Like something's out there watching. I look into the woods and I don't see anything, but it's almost like it silently calls to me. Like something alive." She withdrew her hand from his and took a drink of her coffee. "I told you you'd think I was crazy."

Paul stared at her for a couple of seconds, and Ginny could tell he was contemplating her words. "You're wrong," he said finally. "I still don't think you're crazy."

"You don't have to humor me."

"I'm not humoring you. I think you're sensing something. Some people are very intuitive. If things feel different to you now from how they did before, then something has changed. The fact that it's not immediately visible is disconcerting, but hardly proof that you're imagining it."

He frowned. "And besides, you're forgetting a huge point in your favor."

"What's that?"

"Someone broke into your apartment. Someone *is* watching."

Ginny crossed her arms across her chest as a chill passed over her. "What do they want?"

"I think if we can figure out the why, we may be able to figure out the who."

"We...?" Private detective, she reminded herself. "Oh, but I don't have the money to pay you—"

"I don't want any money," he interrupted. "I just want to help."

Ginny sighed. "You're hoping I'll remember something about your sister."

"I'd be foolish not to hope, but I meant what I said about helping you. Even if your past doesn't help me at all, I'm not going to leave you to deal with whatever is going on. I'll help you find the truth, if you're willing to work with me."

"What would I have to do?"

"Involve me in your life, for starters. I can't watch things closely if we're polite strangers."

"But how? Everyone knows the only family I have

is Madelaine, and I don't want her to know anything about this at all. She'd worry herself to death, and it might all be nothing."

Paul nodded. "A family connection wasn't exactly the kind I had in mind."

Ginny felt a flush run up her neck and onto her face. "You want me to pretend we have a romantic relationship?" She shook her head. "I don't think I can do that. I'm not the relationship kind."

"That makes two of us, but all you have to do is pretend for a bit."

Ginny's mind screamed at her to say no. To walk away from the table and pretend she'd never laid eyes on Paul Stanton, but her body had responded to Paul's suggestion in a completely different way—one that made Ginny's mind scream even more. "What exactly would I have to do, to pretend, that is?"

"That we met at the café, chatted and enjoyed each other's company. I already told your mother I was here on vacation. There's nothing wrong with a little vacation romance."

"I don't think anyone will buy that." Paul, with his toned body, wavy brown hair and supersexy green eyes, was the kind of man who could have anyone. No way would anyone believe he'd chosen her.

Paul looked at her, his confusion clear. "Are you gay?"

"No. I just…I don't think I'm the kind of girl someone like you would be interested in."

"Are you kidding me? You're beautiful." He stared at her for a minute, then shook his head. "You really don't know that, do you?"

Ginny looked down at her watch, not saying a word.

He rose from the booth. "I better get out of here and let you get to the festival before your mother starts worrying. I know we still have a lot to talk about, but we can get to it later. I want you to act completely normal. I don't want anyone to know that you are on to them."

Ginny nodded, still stunned from Paul's earlier declaration.

"I'll drop by the booth when you're not busy. In the meantime, I'll be around, watching." He pulled a card from his pocket and handed it to her. "That card has my cell number on it. If you see anything suspicious or get that feeling like you're being watched, call me immediately."

He pulled some money out of his wallet and handed it to her. "When you see your mother, please tell her the breakfast was great." He exited the café and walked down the sidewalk toward the town square.

Ginny stared after him for a minute, then jumped up and locked the café door behind him.

He'd called her beautiful.

That almost scared her more than knowing someone was watching her.

PAUL WALKED AMONG THE booths of the festival, stopping occasionally to chat with townspeople about their wares and then making notes on his phone to go over with Ginny later on. Whoever was watching Ginny was probably someone local—someone she'd known her entire life, which was why they weren't on her radar. Someone who knew the truth about the past had sensed a change in Ginny or perhaps misread an action and now feared her memory was returning.

And that could be very dangerous for Ginny, especially if something nefarious had gone down at the LeBlanc School all those years ago. Paul believed something was wrong with the entire situation, the school, the girls with no families to speak of, the fire—all of it reeked to high heaven. Someone was already watching her, had already risked getting caught in her apartment. They'd taken that risk for a good reason.

With any luck, he'd figure it out before Ginny's watcher escalated to something worse than reading her journal.

He had to make sure that no one suspected his involvement in researching Ginny's past. In small towns, people would notice everything, especially a stranger dating a local. He had to make sure people believed he was interested in Ginny in the dating sort of way, despite being as averse to relationships as Ginny claimed to be.

He'd meant it when he told her she was beautiful. She was, in fact, one of the most beautiful women he'd ever seen outside of television or magazines. Even without the benefit of camera filters and Photoshop, her skin was flawless, her hair so silky it made him want to touch it. And the eyes. Her eyes were more than just brilliant pools of blue. They conveyed emotion without words.

Get a grip!

The words echoed through his mind. The last thing in the world he should be doing right now is running down a laundry list of Ginny Bergeron's most attractive qualities. He needed to get as much information as he could from her, figure out what the threat to her was and eliminate it, then get out of Johnson's Bayou and back on with his life.

He looked over at Ginny's booth, which had been crowded the entire day. Two women who'd been deliberating over the selection for almost a half hour finally made their choices and left Ginny's table with satisfied looks on their faces. It was the first time that day her booth had been empty, so he walked over to check in. Ginny looked up from her cash box as he approached and gave him a tentative smile.

"Busy today," he said. There were more bare gaps on the table than jewelry.

"Definitely. I'm glad I made extra pieces earlier this week, or I'd run out before the festival is over."

"How long does it last?"

"One more day."

"Good. I can get a rundown on the locals from you tonight, and hopefully some of them will still be around tomorrow so I can get a feel for the ones that interest me."

Ginny looked taken aback. "You think someone who lives here has been spying on me?"

"If it was a stranger, you would have already noticed him."

"Yes, of course. I'm sorry. I must sound stupid, but all of this is so outside of my normal realm."

"Don't worry. It's not outside of mine. I can explain to you how I work tonight."

"What about tonight?" Madelaine's voice sounded behind Paul.

He turned and gave her a smile as she stepped up to Ginny's table. "I was just trying to convince Ginny to let me buy her dinner tonight."

Madelaine beamed at Paul. "That's so nice. Isn't that nice, Ginny?" She poked Ginny, who looked remarkably guilty for a woman who hadn't done anything wrong.

"Yes," Ginny said, coming alive when her mother's finger connected with her ribs. "That would be very nice."

"I know a couple of wonderful restaurants in New Orleans, if you're up for the drive."

"Oh, I have to be at work early. Can we eat in town at Maude's?"

"Sorry. I forgot you guys are up before the chickens. I can pick you up at your place."

"You can meet me at my place. Maude's is just a couple blocks away. I won't be done here until six, though, so it will have to be seven or after."

"Seven is fine. Where is your place?"

"I have an apartment above the café."

Paul smiled. "Seven, then. Nice seeing you again," he said to Madelaine and left.

Madelaine's timing had been perfect. Paul had no doubt that the proud mother would share her daughter's date with her friends. By tomorrow morning, the entire town would know that he'd taken Ginny to dinner, and his alibi would be in place.

He had a couple of hours until he met Ginny, and he needed to get some work done. First up was making a few phone calls about the girl who'd been taken to the hospital in New Orleans after the fire at the LeBlanc School. He'd helped a woman track down her deadbeat ex about six months ago, and if memory served him correct, her mother was a nurse at that hospital. If her daughter referred him, the mother might be willing to talk to him off the record.

If he could find the hospitalized girl—if she was still alive—he might have another lead.

GINNY NERVOUSLY SMOOTHED her skirt under the table at the only restaurant in Johnson's Bayou that was open nights. Paul studied the menu of home cooking and looked far too handsome and polished to be in this town. He wore tan slacks and a navy shirt that looked good next to his tanned skin. He hadn't shaved, and the two-day growth gave his jaw that rugged look that she found so incredibly sexy. Of course, in Johnson's Bayou, she usually saw it only on television, not sitting across the table from her at Aunt Maude's Country Kitchen.

"It's more crowded than I expected," Paul said.

"It's because of the festival."

Paul glanced around the restaurant and frowned. "I don't want to be overheard," he said, his voice low. "Once the table next to us leaves, I'll tell you what I've found."

"Okay. So what do we do in the meantime?"

Paul smiled. "We chat like any other date. Is it really that hard to pretend you're on a date with me? I must need to work on my charm."

Ginny felt a blush rise up her face. "No, it's not you. Johnson's Bayou is not exactly a hotbed of eligible men. I don't date much." *Try not at all.*

"Oh, c'mon. What about those two brothers who own the auto garage? I met them today and they said they were single."

Ginny giggled. The Moreau brothers were in their

mid-eighties, at best. "They're a little too wild for my taste."

Paul laughed. "You know, you're probably right. They told me some whoppers over a burger and beer."

Ginny leaned a bit across the table. "Is that what you did today? Talked to townspeople to get information?"

The family at the table next to them rose from their seats and Paul motioned his head in their direction. Once they were out of earshot, Paul said, "Mostly listened. Small-town people tend to close up if you ask too many questions. One thing that you can probably answer is why the school is still standing. I was surprised to find it, figuring it would have been torn down, especially given the circumstances."

"The house is owned by some real estate trust. The mayor appealed to the trust's lawyers to tear it down, but the house is outside city limits, so he couldn't force them to. I don't think they wanted to absorb the cost. There are a lot of abandoned structures out in the bayou. Eventually the swamp claims them."

"I guess so."

"So did you find out anything by listening?"

"There are a couple of people I wanted to ask you about, but first I want you to tell me about the break-in at your apartment. Did you report it to the sheriff?"

"No. There was no break-in, per se. But I know someone had been in the apartment."

"Was anything missing?"

Ginny shook her head. "But my journal was out of place. I put it in the same place in my nightstand every night."

Paul didn't look convinced. "Are you sure it was

moved? With the festival and your run-in with me in the woods, maybe you didn't follow your usual protocol."

"I know I put it back in the same place, and the bookmark was wrong, too. Even if I got one wrong, I wouldn't have messed up both. Besides, there was a faint smell of men's cologne, and I don't have anything in the apartment that smells musky." She hesitated for a moment, not wanting to say what was on the tip of her tongue.

Paul narrowed his eyes at her. "Whatever you're thinking you shouldn't tell me, I wish you would."

"Is mind reading one of your skills?"

"No, but a good detective is perceptive and knows to watch body language. Yours tells me you're holding something back."

Ginny sighed. "I know you've already said you don't think I'm crazy, but this is still going to sound odd. I know someone was in the apartment because it felt different. From the moment I walked in the door, something felt off, almost ominous."

"But nothing was missing and nothing was out of place except the journal?"

"Yeah." Ginny looked at Paul, trying to read him as he'd read her, but all she saw was a man contemplating her words.

"Okay," he said finally. "If you definitely think someone was in your apartment and read your journal, then I believe that's exactly what happened. It fits, really, if we assume someone is afraid you're remembering. If you were, your journal is where you'd document those thoughts."

"But there's nothing in there. I mean, nothing concrete. I wrote about feeling unsettled lately, but what girl in her twenties working for her mother and living in a tiny town wouldn't feel that way?" Except her. Until someone started watching.

"He'll be thinking of everything in terms of what he wants to hide. If he was involved in anything that happened at the LeBlanc School, he's not young. His mind won't automatically go to the norm for young ladies."

He pulled his phone from his pocket. "I jotted down a couple of names today that I wanted to ask you about. The first one is Saul Pritchard."

"He's a handyman. Does basic repair and maintenance for the people and businesses in town."

"Did he work at the LeBlanc School?"

"Yes."

"Did you see him there?"

"I don't remember ever being at the house before the other night. If I saw him there, I don't remember. I'm sure I've heard someone in town say he worked there, but I don't remember who it was. People here don't talk much about the LeBlanc School."

"Which is interesting in itself. Usually that sort of thing is huge gossip in small towns."

Ginny frowned. "I think it's because it was kids. The whole thing is horrifying, and I think a lot of people are embarrassed because something was going on under their noses and they never have figured out what. They're the same way with me."

"What do you mean?"

"People here are suspicious. The rumors range from I'm the child of a witch to I was meant to be a sacrifice that escaped. Just my presence makes a lot of people uneasy. And I don't help matters. I never had friends in school—mostly because the other kids avoided me—but I keep to myself as an adult, too. Then, when I turned down a college scholarship, some decided that I'd been cursed and couldn't leave the town."

"Wow. Big imaginations some people have."

Ginny shrugged. "They're simple people. Things they don't have an answer for scare them."

"There's another reason they might be scared."

"What's that?"

"Some of them were involved, and they don't want anyone to figure out what was going on."

"Yeah. I'm sure you're right. I just hate to think—"

"Ginny." A man's voice boomed across the restaurant.

Ginny looked over and saw the mayor of Johnson's Bayou making his way over to her table, his wife and two disgruntled teenagers in tow. She forced a smile on her face.

"Hello," she said as Mayor Daigle stepped up to the table.

"My wife said you're doing a brisk business at the festival." He glanced over at Paul, the curiosity clear on his face.

"Yes," Ginny said. "I've been doing very well."

The mayor looked over at Paul again, then back at Ginny, clearly not about to leave until she made an introduction.

"Oh, sorry," Ginny said. "Mayor Daigle, this is Paul Stanton. He's here for the festival and some fishing."

Mayor Daigle turned to Paul and extended his hand. "Joe Daigle," he said as Paul shook his hand. "Stanton, huh? Any relation to Emily Stanton in Lafayette?"

"Not that I'm aware of," Paul replied.

Mayor Daigle waited, clearly hoping Paul would give him more information, but Paul just smiled pleasantly.

"Well, enjoy your vacation," Mayor Daigle said finally. "I'll let you kids get back to your dinner." His wife said a hasty goodbye and followed her husband and teens out of the restaurant.

"Is the mayor always so nosy?" Paul asked.

"Yes. My mom says he had two options for a career—politician or gossip columnist."

"Hmm. I wonder if I could get him to talk about the school?"

"Anything's possible. He'll be fishing early tomorrow morning at his favorite spot. You could always pretend to run into him and give it a shot."

"Good idea." He glanced around the restaurant and leaned across the table toward Ginny. "I have another idea. I want to go back to the school tonight."

Chapter Six

"No." Ginny's response was immediate and one she didn't have to give a second's thought to. "I'm not going back there. The place frightens me, and clearly, I'm not mentally sound when I'm there, since I heard screaming that didn't exist."

"We don't know for sure it didn't happen."

"I do. If a child was missing from the town, I would have heard about it at the café."

"Not necessarily."

"Even if the child wasn't from here, someone would have come looking."

"I don't think a child was in the woods the other night."

"Then we're right back to my being mental."

Paul shook his head. "I think being in the woods triggered a memory in you. One so strong that you thought you'd just heard it."

Ginny sat back in her chair, her mind trying to process what Paul was suggesting. It was absurd, yet on some level, it almost made sense. "So I'm not crazy— I'm just having incredibly lucid recall? Do you really think that's possible?"

"Yes. And I think going back may trigger more memories."

Ginny pulled at a loose thread on her napkin, torn by her desire to help Paul find his sister and her own fear of what remembering the past may bring to her own life. The truth of what happened at the LeBlanc School that night had to be ugly, but what about her own past? What if she found out things about her life before that night that changed the way she felt about her life now?

Her temples began to throb as her pulse spiked. She looked across the table at Paul, and her heart broke just a little at the hopeful look that stared back at her. Refusing would be selfish. Refusing would mean she was allowing fear to dictate how she lived, and that was something she wasn't prepared to do.

"I'll do it," she said before she could change her mind.

GINNY SLIPPED OUT THE back door of the café behind Paul, clutching her spotlight, and crossed the alley, where they paused a minute in the shadows. They'd both changed into jeans, tennis shoes and dark shirts to help camouflage themselves in the darkness, and now they stepped into the field between the woods and the alley and headed away from town. At first they traveled in a different direction from the place where Ginny had entered the swamp before, choosing instead to stick to the dark gap between the town's streetlights. Midway across the field, when the town's lights no longer reached them, they turned and headed for the trail where Ginny had entered the woods before.

Ginny paused in front of the wall of trees, every

instinct in her body telling her to run back inside and lock the doors behind her. She took a deep breath and blew it out slowly, then passed her spotlight to Paul and nodded. He entered the woods and she stepped in behind him, waiting until they were a good twenty feet into the gloomy darkness before he turned on the light.

The spotlight immediately changed the look of the swamp but didn't reduce Ginny's feeling of foreboding one bit. The cypress trees, heavy with moss, still closed in on her like a tomb, making her chest feel heavy, almost as if she was suffocating. She concentrated on her breathing, making sure it was steady and deep.

"You okay?" Paul asked.

"Yeah. How much farther?"

"About a hundred yards or so."

"That far?" Ginny glanced behind her at the wall of trees and moss. She couldn't see even a flicker of light from town, and the sky overhead was dark with clouds so that not even a sliver of moonlight was showing. She hadn't realized she'd run that far into the woods that night, and she barely remembered her dash out, either.

"It just feels far," Paul said. "Don't worry. I'm with you every step."

"Do you have that big gun with you?"

Paul lifted his shirt to expose the pistol tucked into his waistband. "I don't leave home without it."

Ginny nodded and he continued through the brush. As she walked, Ginny wondered what had happened that night, sixteen years ago. She remembered nothing at all about her life before waking up in the hospital a week after the fire. Madelaine told her she'd walked out of the woods right in the middle of the fire trucks as if she didn't see or hear anything around her. The paramedics said she was in shock and rushed her to the hospital in New Orleans.

Could Paul be right? Was she starting to remember?

She watched the ground closely as she walked. The last thing she needed was to twist an ankle in the gnarled roots that covered the swamp floor or, even worse, have a run-in with one of the poisonous varieties of snakes that liked to hunt at night. One, two, three…she counted her steps as she walked. It distracted her very creative mind.

All of a sudden, the woods went completely dark. She almost ran into Paul before she realized he'd stopped walking and had turned off the spotlight. "What's wrong?" she whispered.

"We're at the edge of the clearing surrounding the house," he said, his voice low. "I wanted to watch and listen for a minute before we entered the house."

Ginny sucked in a breath. "You think someone might be in there?"

"No, but I wouldn't be doing my job if I didn't think about those things."

Ginny let the breath out, her anxiety lessening a bit. Paul was a detective. He would be naturally cautious. She stepped beside him and peered into the darkness toward the school. The cloudy skies made it impossible to make out more than the rooflines of the structure, which jutted up against the black sky. Stilling herself, she focused on listening instead. The sound of the night creatures sounded around them, but nothing out of the ordinary reached her ears. And more important, nothing predatory—animal or human.

Apparently satisfied as well, Paul turned on the spotlight and motioned to Ginny as he stepped out of the brush and into the clearing surrounding the school. He picked up the pace across the clearing and into the front entry of the house, then stopped inside.

"I looked around a little the other night, but only a cursory check to make sure the child you heard wasn't here. All the bedrooms for the girls were upstairs. I figured we could start there."

"Okay," Ginny said and followed Paul up the sweeping circular staircase to the second-floor hallway. Starting with the bedrooms made sense. If she'd lived at the school, she'd probably spent more time in her bedroom than anywhere else.

They stepped into the first room and Paul shone the spotlight up at the ceiling, which cast a glow over the entire room. Ginny made a first pass around the small space and frowned. The room contained two twin beds, still covered with ruffled comforters and matching pillows. The material was dirty now and had been torn and picked over in spots, most likely by rodents looking for good nest-building material, but the pink fabric still showed in some places. Children's books lay on the nightstand positioned between the two beds, and a tattered rug lay on the floor in front of the nightstand. A dresser stood behind her and she tugged on the top drawer, which seemed to stick.

"It's probably stuck." Paul stepped close to her and pulled on the drawer handle. The drawer popped open and mice ran out of the top and scattered over the dresser and out of the room.

"Oh," Ginny jumped back from the dresser and

checked her feet, making sure none of the rodents were running across them.

Paul stepped back beside her. "I should have thought about that. Sorry."

"At least none of them ran across my shoes. Then I would have had to burn a perfectly good pair of Nikes."

Paul gave her a rueful smile. "There's still plenty of opportunity. We need to check all the drawers. See if there's anything here that might give us an indication of what happened."

Ginny glanced around the room again. "Why is everything still here? Some of the furniture has to be valuable, or must have been at one time, but it's all sat here untouched. It's creepy."

"Yeah. It kinda surprised me, too. I figured someone looking to make a quick buck would have picked it over years ago."

"Maybe not," Ginny said. "The New Orleans newspaper carried the story about the fire, but it never made national news that I can recall. Only people from Johnson's Bayou knew that the police never identified a next of kin or even a friend of the headmistress. I believe some company in New Orleans owns the property, although they clearly didn't care enough to sell off the assets."

"Not having a legal right to things doesn't stop people from looting."

"Oh, people in Johnson's Bayou don't avoid the house because they're afraid of breaking the law."

"Then what are they afraid of?"

Ginny shrugged. "I don't know exactly. I heard the whispers when I was a child. People thought the headmistress was a witch and the girls were sacrificed in some ritual. Given that her body was never found and she's completely disappeared, people are more willing to believe the extraordinary."

"Is it extraordinary?"

Ginny stared at Paul. "You're serious? You believe in witchcraft?"

"No, but I believe that some people believe in witchcraft. If the headmistress was one of them, then the locals' suspicions might have merit."

"Then what happened to her?"

"The easy answer—she became someone else. New identity, new past, new town."

Ginny shook her head, just beginning to realize how many questions needed to be answered about that night. How many avenues of investigation Paul might have to pursue before he got the answers he sought. "Then I guess we better get a move on. There's a lot of things we don't know."

Paul pulled open all the drawers on the dresser and the nightstand, but no other four-legged surprises jumped out at them. He placed the spotlight on top of the dresser with the light still shining on the ceiling to illuminate the room and pulled a flashlight from his back pocket. "I'm going to start on the next room. Are you okay in here?"

"As long as everything in the room is bipedal, I'm fine."

"I'll open the drawers next door before you check out the room, then I'll start searching the rooms across the hall. Yell if you find anything interesting."

Ginny nodded and began to pull clothes out of the dresser drawers. They were dry-rotted, and many of them crumbled in places when she pulled them from their resting spot. She cringed a bit when she saw bugs on the end of the garment, but when she realized they were dead, she flicked them off with her fingernail. Carefully, she felt each garment for anything that might be hidden inside, and when the drawer was empty, she stuffed all the clothes back inside and moved on to the next drawer, repeating the process.

The dresser yielded nothing at all of interest and Ginny moved to the nightstand. The nightstand drawer held a stack of fabric and a box of thread. Ginny pulled the stack out and opened up the square piece of cloth with the neat hem. It was dingy and rotting, but the square was the same as the blue gingham valances in the café. Ginny felt a lump in her throat and choked it down. They were normal little girls who worked on their sewing and reading books before going to bed.

What had they felt when the fire started? When they realized they were going to die?

She picked up one of the books from the desktop and used the swatch of fabric to wipe the cover. Dust billowed up and she dropped the fabric back in the drawer then waved her hand in front of her face, sneezing as she got a nose full of the dust. She opened the book and looked inside the first page to see if there was an inscription that gave any clue to the owner, but the inside page contained no writing, nor did any of the others.

She picked up the next book and flipped through the pages, not expecting to find anything, when a page toward the end caught her eye. Slowly, she turned the pages back one at a time, trying to figure out what had grabbed her attention. And then she gasped.

It was the design—the circles that she used in her jewelry.

She drew her finger lightly over the circles, the sensitive tip of her finger picking up the tiny difference in texture of the ink used to draw the circles. Paul had been right. The circles came from her past. And now she knew for certain that she'd been in the LeBlanc School. But had she drawn the circles in the book or had someone else, maybe Paul's sister?

She flipped the book back to the front cover and studied the title and artwork. It wasn't familiar. Not a single thing fired in her mind that let her know she'd seen the book before. Frustrated, she closed the book. She needed to show it to Paul and get his thoughts. He had a way of making sense out of this mess.

As she turned to leave the room, the window behind her shattered and she felt something whiz by her head. Before she could even register what had happened, Paul rushed into the room and threw her to the floor as another pane of glass shattered behind them. She covered her head with her arms, the shards of broken glass nicking her bare skin as it fell around them.

Paul had covered most of her body with his own when he'd tackled her, but now he moved to his hands and knees. "Get into the hallway. Do not stand." He motioned for her to get ahead of him, so Ginny crawled out of the room and into the hallway, where she slumped against the wall on the other side of the bedroom door.

The spotlight in the bedroom clicked off and the entire hallway pitched into darkness, not even a sliver of light making its way in. A couple of seconds later, Paul placed the spotlight on the floor next to her and turned on his small flashlight. He pulled his pistol from his waistband and checked the clip.

"Someone was shooting at me," Ginny said, everything that had just happened suddenly falling into place. "But I didn't hear a shot."

"He's using a silencer. Gunfire would attract attention."

"I can't believe it. Why in the world would anyone shoot at me?"

Paul hesitated for a moment, then replied, "Because they have a lot to lose if your memory returns."

He rose from the floor and clicked off his flashlight, pitching the hallway back into darkness. "Stay put and keep the spotlight off."

Ginny squinted up into the black, but Paul was only a vague outline. "Where are you going?" she asked, trying to keep the panic from her voice.

"To see if I can figure out where that shot came from. We have to get out of the house without him seeing."

"But he could be anywhere. He could have moved already."

"I know, but we're sitting ducks here. Just stay quiet and if you hear anyone moving downstairs, yell."

Ginny's grip tightened on something in her hands, and she realized with a start that it was the children's book, the one with the circle designs drawn in it. The book had been completely forgotten in the wake of the gunfire and exploding glass.

She sat in the darkness, listening for any sound that indicated someone was moving in the house, but even Paul had slipped into silence. Occasionally, she heard the sound of tiny scurrying feet and hoped all the four-legged creatures were far away and the sound was echoing in the cavernous hallway. The darkness closed in on her and she felt her panic rise. How were they going to get out of the house? There were probably multiple exits, but they had no way of knowing where the shooter was.

Or if he was alone.

Ginny sucked in a breath. They could be surrounded. They could die in here and no one would ever know what happened. No one would ever suspect that Ginny and the handsome stranger had ventured into the woods at night to search the LeBlanc School. And even if the sheriff eventually decided to look here, their bodies would be long gone, along with any trace that they'd been in the rotting structure.

Why had she agreed to come here tonight? In hindsight, it was the dumbest thing she'd ever done. Well, maybe second dumbest, since coming the first time had set everything in motion.

"Ginny." Paul's whisper sounded next to her and she pressed her hand over her mouth to strangle a cry.

He stooped down and placed his hand on her shoulder. "There's a staircase at the end of the hall that leads to the kitchen below. There's an exit door off the kitchen."

"But what if he sees us?"

"The exit in the kitchen is only twenty feet from the edge of the swamp and there's a storage building in between. If we can make it across, we have a good chance of losing him in the swamp."

"What if he's not alone?"

"It's a chance we have to take. If we stay here, he

will find us. I have a plan that will buy us some time, I hope."

Ginny rose from the floor, still clutching the book. She knew he was right, but it was the last thing she wanted to hear.

"Give me a couple of minutes and I'll be right back," Paul said.

Ginny squinted, trying to make out his shape in the dim hall. He'd gone toward the main staircase, which didn't make sense. He'd said they were going to use the rear staircase. All of a sudden, she heard something in the direction Paul had gone. It sounded like glass clinking together. A second later, she saw the glow of the small flashlight on the landing, partially illuminating Paul as he secured the flashlight to a chandelier just above the railing.

He hurried back to Ginny and whispered, "Let's go, and no talking until we're safe."

Ginny clutched a handful of the back of his shirt in one hand and the book in the other and slipped down the hallway after Paul, praying that the old floor didn't creak as they walked. They made it to the end of the hallway and Paul stopped a minute and put a finger to his lips. He listened for a moment then pointed at the stairwell. Keeping a death grip on his shirt, she followed him down the stairs into the kitchen.

The exterior door was just beyond the staircase, and Ginny huddled beside Paul as he twisted the doorknob and leaned on the door. But it didn't budge. He looked back at Ginny, and she could barely make out the worried expression on his face. If he had to force the door open, it would make a lot of noise.

He leaned close to her and whispered, "Prepare to run."

Ginny nodded and said a silent prayer that the shooter was on the far side of the clearing. Paul placed his shoulder against the door, then froze. He looked at her and pointed in the direction of the front entry of the house. She thought for a moment he was telling her they would exit by the front entry instead, but then she heard it—the sound of the front door opening. She heard someone curse and then the sound of footsteps running up the main stairwell.

The flashlight! The shooter had followed the light on the chandelier into the front of the house and was now running upstairs. Paul's plan had worked. Paul tapped her and motioned to the door just as the footsteps hit the second-floor landing, then he thrust his shoulder into the kitchen door and it flew open with a screech.

Chapter Seven

Paul grabbed her hand and ran out of the kitchen for the swamp. Ginny ran as fast as possible, alternating between praying there was nothing to trip over in the dark and listening for the sound of the shooter behind them. When they hit the woods, Paul dropped her hand for better maneuverability but barely slowed as he angled off in the swamp in the opposite direction of town. Ginny pulled on his arm, trying to let him know they were going in the wrong direction, but he paused only long enough to shake his head and then pick up the pace again.

She hesitated just a second then followed him deep into the swamp. The sound of the kitchen door slamming against the side of the house echoed through the swamp and Paul picked up the pace. She held the book up to protect her face as she ran, and the brush tore at the bare skin on her arms. At one point, she heard the sound of cloth ripping, but there was no time to think about it.

Her thighs and calves burned from the exertion, and her breathing grew labored every second that they continued at full speed. Sheer adrenaline kept her pushing forward, and she knew that if she lived to see tomorrow, her body would make sure she paid for the abuse. Just as she wondered how much longer she could sustain the pace, they burst into a clearing that contained a tiny, rundown cabin.

The moon cleared a patch of clouds and cast a dim glow around the cabin as Paul ran for the truck that was parked on the side. He paused only long enough to retrieve keys from under the wheel well and jumped inside. Bewildered, Ginny jumped into the passenger's side of the truck, and a second later Paul tore out of the clearing down a narrow path to town.

"Stay down," he said.

The words hadn't quite finished leaving his mouth when Ginny heard the cracking of glass. Immediately, she slumped in her seat and looked up to see a small hole in the back windshield of the truck, not even an inch from where her head had been only moments before.

Paul crouched so low in his seat that Ginny worried he could even see where he was going. She heard another pop and saw a second hole appear. She slid down until she rested on the floorboard, praying that Paul wouldn't wreck the truck on his way out of the swamp. Her heart pounded so loudly in her chest that she felt it would burst.

"Hold on!" Paul said as he made a sharp right-hand turn.

Ginny dropped the book on the floorboard and clutched the seat, struggling to keep from falling from the momentum of the turn.

"You can get up," Paul said once they were going straight again.

Ginny crawled up on the seat and let her breath out

with a whoosh. Her pulse raced and she took several deep breaths, trying to calm her nervous system.

"Are you all right?" Paul asked. "Do you have any injuries?"

"No," Ginny said. "Scratches from running through the swamp, but nothing serious except for the heart attack I may have when I'm able to process everything that just happened."

Paul placed his hand on hers and gave it a squeeze. "If you're able to make a joke, you're a lot stronger than you realize. Most people wouldn't have been able to handle this as well."

Ginny felt a bit proud at Paul's words. She'd never considered herself particularly brave or strong. Average had been her own assessment, but maybe Paul was right. Maybe she had untapped strength resting just under the surface.

"Thank you," she said, "but if it takes being shot at to show my strength, I think I'll just go back to normal."

Paul frowned. "I'm afraid your life isn't going to return to normal until we figure out what's going on here. Whoever shot at us was either anticipating you visiting the house and staking it out or was following us. I was very watchful. I don't think he followed us there."

"I shouldn't have gone back to the house. Now, he thinks I remember something, and I don't."

"He already thought you remembered something, or he wouldn't have been waiting. I'm sorry, Ginny, but you would have been in danger even if you hadn't gone to the house. He was already watching you, or he wouldn't have broken into your apartment and read your journal. Something in your behavior must have changed and caused him to pay closer attention to you."

"But he escalated because we went to the house. Maybe if I'd stopped journaling my thoughts about the house and hidden my feelings, he would have gone away, like he has for the past sixteen years."

Paul was silent, and Ginny knew he was thinking about what she'd said. "Hey, I didn't mean for you to feel guilty," she said. "I was already going to the house before tonight. That's why I'd bought the spotlight." She sighed. "If you hadn't been with me, he could have easily killed me and no one would ever have known what happened."

Ginny stared out the windshield as Paul pulled into town, then buried her head in her hands. "What am I going to do? It wasn't supposed to go like this."

Paul parked in front of the café and placed his hand on Ginny's back. "Hey, we'll figure it out. I promise."

Ginny straightened up and nodded.

"We should get inside," Paul said.

The terror she'd felt earlier washed over her in a giant wave, and Ginny jumped out of the truck and hurried over to the front door of the café. She fumbled in her jeans pocket for her keys, and her hands shook as she tried to place the key in the lock. She dropped the keys and cursed.

Before she could bend over, Paul picked up the keys. "Let me," he said and unlocked the door.

Ginny pushed the door open and rushed inside, pulling Paul behind her. She twisted the dead bolt back into place then hurried through the café and up the staircase to her apartment, not even looking to see if

Paul followed. When she reached the apartment door, she realized Paul still had her keys. Before she could call out, he stepped on the landing behind her and passed her the keys.

This time, her hand was steadier and she managed the lock on her own, but as soon as she stepped inside the apartment, she stopped, unable to think or move. She heard Paul close and lock the door behind her, then he gently took her by the elbow and guided her to the couch to sit. He left immediately and she could hear him rummaging through her kitchen, but she didn't even have the desire to turn and see what he was doing.

A minute later, he handed her a glass. "Drink," he instructed and took her hands in his, gliding the glass to her lips.

She took a drink and grimaced at the bitter taste of the whiskey. It burned a little going down her throat, but she took another gulp then leaned back on the couch, trying to calm her frantic mind. Paul placed the glass on the coffee table and sat next to her, his worried eyes studying her face.

"You're in shock," he said. "Don't try to talk. Just relax for a minute and let the whiskey do its job."

Ginny nodded and leaned back on the couch, closing her eyes. She felt the whiskey begin to warm in her belly and move up her body. Her muscles began to relax and her heartbeat slowed to an almost normal pace. She opened her eyes and found Paul anxiously watching her.

"I'm sorry I worried you," she said.

"Don't you dare apologize. Tonight scared me, and I've got eight years of being a cop and two of being a private investigator behind me."

"What are we going to do? This is my home. I don't know anything else but I don't feel safe here anymore."

"Who else has a key to your apartment?"

"Only Mom."

"No landlord?"

"No. Mom bought the building several years back from some ritzy attorney in New Orleans. I think he owned several buildings here."

"Okay, but if the shooter didn't force entry in here to read your journal, someone else besides Madelaine must have a key. Did you keep a spare in the café?"

"No. Only two keys came with the lock. I took one and gave Mom the other."

"Who installed the lock?"

Ginny sucked in a breath. "Saul Pritchard. You asked me about him earlier. Do you think he could be behind this? Was there some way he could have duplicated the key?"

"I don't know, but I'm going to have my partner do some checking on Mr. Pritchard. See what he can dig up." Paul rose from the couch. "But for now, I think you ought to take a hot shower, see to those scratches and try to get some sleep."

"Yeah, sure. Like I'm going to sleep knowing someone has a key to my apartment."

"The inside dead bolt is locked, and I'm not moving off that couch until morning."

Ginny stared. "Oh, no. I can't let you stay."

"You don't have a choice. I'm not leaving. I know you were already headed down this line of searching, but I still feel responsible for upping the stakes. I'm not leaving you unprotected until we find out what's going on."

Ginny stiffened. "I appreciate your sense of responsibility, but I am not helpless. This is a small town. I can hardly have some man I've just met staying with me. Remember, I have to live here long after you're gone."

"I'm not trying to get you cast with a scarlet letter. I'll sneak out in the morning before anyone can see."

"So you'll be leaving before 5:00 a.m., then?"

Paul blanched. "I thought the café didn't open until six?"

"It doesn't, but my mom gets here early to start baking. You didn't think those cinnamon rolls came out of a can, did you?"

Paul sighed. "I guess not. I'll be out of here at four-thirty. Just to be safe. But I'm going to park my truck somewhere that I can still see the café."

Ginny jumped up. "The book! I left the book in the truck."

"What book?"

"I found it at the school. I was on my way to show you when the shooting started. It's a children's book and it has the circle design penciled on a page inside. We have to go get the book."

"No. We have to stay inside where it's safe. The most logical place to look for us is here. No one is walking outside and giving him an easy shot."

"But what if he steals it?"

"If you say it was the same design, I believe you."

"So that means your sister was there, right? That I got the design from her at the school?"

Paul frowned. "I wish it were that simple."

"But what else could it possibly be?"

"Maybe she was at the school, or maybe you met her

somewhere else before the LeBlanc School and you're the one who drew it in the book. We don't know how you got here, so we don't know where you were before, and since you can't remember what happened at the school…"

Ginny's excitement over the find deflated. "Oh. I guess you're right."

"Don't be disappointed," Paul said, cluing in to her mood. "It proves you were there, at least, which is more than we could be certain of before tonight. I'll check the book tomorrow and see if I can lift prints off the inside page."

"But my prints are on it, now."

"Your fingerprints will be the same, but bigger as an adult. An expert can easily differentiate the two."

"That's assuming it's still in the truck in the morning. So I guess the truck is yours? When we were racing away from that cabin, I thought for a minute you'd stolen someone's truck, but then I remembered you knew where the key was. Why was it parked at that cabin?"

"It's my truck. The hotel was full because of the festival. I thought I'd have to drive back and forth from New Orleans, but my partner knew a guy who owned that fishing cabin, so I stayed there."

"So you walked into town to meet me for dinner?" Ginny narrowed her eyes at him. "You were expecting trouble. That's why you left your truck there."

"I was *preparing* for trouble, not expecting. Preparing is part of my job."

Ginny felt the anger that had started to develop dissipate at his perfectly reasonable explanation, but just a bit of annoyance remained. Paul seemed to be one step ahead of her on everything, and it made her uncomfortable. Of course, he was also one step ahead of the shooter, and she couldn't exactly argue the value of that.

"If we're going to work together on this," she said, "you're going to have to tell me everything. Every plan, every preparation. I don't want to feel like you're leaving things out or that I can't trust you."

Paul nodded. "I'll tell you everything I know. Unfortunately, right now you're completely up to speed."

By the frustration in his expression, Ginny knew he was telling her the truth, and her heart tugged a little for the man who'd invested so much into looking for the sister he'd lost long ago. "There's extra blankets and a pillow in the bedroom closet. Help yourself to those and anything in the kitchen."

She headed to the shower before she could draw out the conversation any longer. She had too many unanswered questions, too many emotions coursing through her, and Paul Stanton sleeping on her couch was only adding to the mix.

She needed to put some distance between them, even if it was only ten feet and a thin interior door.

PAUL WAITED UNTIL HE heard the shower running to pull out his cell phone and call his partner, Mike. It was close to midnight, but Paul wasn't surprised in the least when Mike picked up on the first ring. His partner had vampire tendencies and usually handled the late-night stakeouts.

"Did she remember anything?" Mike asked as soon as he answered.

"No, but she didn't get much of an opportunity to before someone started shooting at her."

"Seriously? Man, that is bad. Real bad. Are you guys okay?"

"Yeah. We both got some scratches running through the swamp, and she was pretty shaken by the time we got back to her apartment, but no serious injuries."

"Not the physical kind, anyway."

Paul ran one hand through his hair. "Yeah. I didn't exactly have scaring her half to death on my list of things to do." Paul cursed. "I hate this! She's agreed to help me against her better judgment, and look what happens the first time out."

Mike was silent for a couple of seconds. "Doesn't matter, really. I know the shooter didn't follow you. You're too careful. So that means he was waiting for you, which means he was already watching her."

"I know. I came around to that when I was barreling through a swamp as fast as I could run and praying I didn't trip over an alligator. But that doesn't mean I have to like it."

"It could have been worse. She was already going down that path when you met her. If you hadn't been there tonight, how much of a chance would she have had?"

Paul walked the couple of steps into the kitchen and poured himself a shot of whiskey. "Not much, and before you ask, she knows all of this and agrees. But I still don't have to like it."

"Of course you don't have to like it. I don't like it, either, but what options do we have now? I'm assuming she won't leave."

"No, and I don't think it would do any good. I'll

never figure all this out without her, and she can't be safe here until I figure it all out."

"Sounds like a mess. I know you didn't call for reassurance, so what do you have for me?"

"A couple of people I want you to check up on. The first is Saul Pritchard. He's in his fifties and worked as a handyman at the school. The second is Thomas Blackwell. He's the sheriff."

"You think the sheriff was involved?"

"Not at this point, but he was the sheriff when the school burned, and he's still sheriff now. I want to know if he has any skeletons that someone could use against him. Last one is Joe Daigle, the mayor."

"I'll bite—why the mayor?"

"Because he's nosy and interrupted my dinner, and neither his kids nor his wife look like they like him very much."

Mike laughed. "Good enough reason for me. That it?"

"Yeah. Call me as soon as you have something."

"Will do, and Paul…be careful."

Paul laid his cell phone on the kitchen counter and poured himself another shot of whiskey. Be careful. That advice was a little late. He'd already endangered himself and his best lead and now he was sharing an apartment with a woman, something he'd sworn he'd never do again after his breakup with the very beautiful and very vengeful Marie.

He tried to tell himself that this was different. That it was business, but he couldn't deny his attraction to Ginny. She was a beautiful woman on the inside and the outside, and in his experience that was rare. She had strength and pride, but no ego. And her vulnerability just drew him to her more.

She doesn't need you to rescue her.

Well, that wasn't exactly true. She *did* need his help with her past, not just her future. And he was going to do everything possible to guarantee she had a good one.

Chapter Eight

Ginny stood next to the couch, the light from the bedroom casting a dim glow over the living room. It was twenty till five and she needed to wake Paul up and get him out of the café before Madelaine arrived. Her mother wanted her to find a man, but if she thought Ginny had brought one home on the first date, she'd have a coronary.

But he looked so handsome sleeping. So serene. In the short time she'd known him, he'd mostly looked angry or worried. Of course, even then, she'd have had to be blind not to see how attractive he was, but when people were shooting at you, you usually didn't stop to compliment a man on how good he looked in jeans.

She shook her head to clear her mind of the instant flash of Paul last night when she'd met him in front of the café for dinner. The last thing she needed was to think about things she couldn't have—things that would complicate an already complicated situation beyond her ability to control it. She was already in neck deep with him. She couldn't afford to drown.

Reaching over, she gently shook his shoulder. "Paul," she called. "Paul, it's time to get up."

He bolted straight up and grabbed her by the wrist.

She gasped at both his speed and the strength of his grip. It took only a second for him to focus and let her go.

"I am so sorry," he said, clearly embarrassed. "You startled me, but I'm not usually this on edge."

"You came by it honest. Being on edge keeps you alert. I need you alert."

His relief was apparent, and Ginny realized it wasn't just relief over grabbing her.

"You're right," he said and rose from the couch and started to fold the blanket.

"Don't worry about the bedding," Ginny said and glanced at the clock.

Paul grinned. "Just get out before Madelaine thinks you're a sinful hussy?"

Ginny smiled. "Something like that."

Paul picked up his keys and cell phone from the coffee table and headed to the front door. He paused on the threshold and turned back to face her. "I'm not going to let him hurt you." Then he turned and hurried down the stairs.

The determination and sincerity in his expression was so clear that it gave her pause for a moment, then she followed him a couple of seconds later to lock the café door behind him. Peering out the back window of the café kitchen, she watched as he hurried down the alley and around the corner of the café.

"Damn," she said as she glanced at her watch then hurried up the stairs to finish getting ready. It was only minutes before Madelaine showed up and she didn't want to be late two days in a row, or her mother would start watching her more closely, too. The last thing she needed was to draw her mother into this mess.

Ginny drew up short at her apartment door and sucked in a breath. Was Madelaine in danger? She hadn't even thought about how this situation might affect her mother. Surely, if Paul thought there was a problem, he would have said so. Unless, of course, he was so distracted by everything else that he hadn't gotten around to that avenue of thought.

Ginny strode into the bathroom and splashed cold water on her face. At first opportunity, she'd ask Paul if he thought Madelaine was in any danger from their investigation. In the meantime, she'd pray his answer was no.

She pulled her hair back in a ponytail and slipped on jeans, a café T-shirt and tennis shoes, then hurried downstairs. Madelaine was just coming through the front door as Ginny stepped into the kitchen.

Madelaine beamed as soon as she saw Ginny and hustled over to the desk to dump her purse on it. "I'm going to put on coffee, and then you're going to tell me all about your date last night."

"Mom, please. There's really nothing to talk about."

Madelaine waved a hand in dismissal. "Nonsense. A handsome young man riding into town and sweeping my daughter off to dinner is the most exciting thing that's happened in years."

"Hmm," Ginny said and started peeling potatoes for hash browns. If Madelaine only knew about the after-dinner happenings, she'd be far less inclined to think a tame dinner was exciting. But if Ginny had any control at all, she was going to make sure that her mother didn't find out a thing until it was all over.

Madelaine filled the last coffeepot and washed her hands before reaching for the flour to start on the cinnamon rolls. "So, are you going to leave me in suspense? Tell me how the dinner was."

"It was nice."

Madelaine sighed. "Fine. I guess I'm going to have to pick it out of you piece by piece. Let's start with work. What does he do for a living?"

Shoot.

Ginny froze. Even though he hadn't come right out and said it, she was certain Paul didn't want anyone to know he was a detective. She searched her mind to come up with something that would satisfy Madelaine.

"He has his own business with a partner—consulting of some sort."

Madelaine nodded. "The smart ones always go out on their own. That's good. I don't want you hooked up with someone stupid."

"Mom! I'm hardly 'hooked up' with him. It was just dinner. In a couple of days, he'll be back in New Orleans and I'll probably never hear from him again." Ginny stared down at the counter and frowned as she delivered that last sentence. It was undoubtedly true, but she was surprised at the momentary flash of disappointment she'd felt when she'd said it.

"Well, you never know. Besides, there's nothing wrong with a nice diversion every now and then. What did you two talk about?"

"Oh, about the festival, fishing…your basic stuff." She looked over at Madelaine and grinned. "Mayor Daigle stopped at the table to introduce himself."

Madelaine snorted. "That old busybody. Thinks he needs to know everything about everybody."

Ginny stopped peeling for a couple of seconds, her mother's words rolling around in her mind. "Mom…

did you ever, I mean, all those years ago…did you ever try to find out where I came from?"

Madelaine looked up from her dough, a surprised look on her face. Ginny could hardly blame her. In all her sixteen years with Madelaine, she couldn't remember even once asking her mother about her past.

"What brought that question on?"

Ginny shrugged, trying to appear nonchalant. "I don't know. I guess when we were talking about family last night, I started thinking that I might have more out there, but there's no way to know."

Madelaine sighed. "You may at that, but if you do, none of them knew about you well enough to come looking for you. The police searched all those databases, but you didn't match a description anywhere. They put your information in the system and ran your picture on the news. Not much else they could do."

Ginny nodded. "But no one had seen me before that day, right? I mean, the students from the LeBlanc School used to come into town, but I wasn't one of them?"

"That day you walked out of the swamp is the first day I ever laid eyes on you. Of that, I'm certain." Madelaine looked at her, the concern evident on her face. "Are you sure you're all right? You've never asked about this."

"I know."

"I'm happy to tell you anything that I know. You don't feel like I've been hiding things from you, do you?"

"Oh, no! That's not it at all. And please don't worry about me. I swear, I rarely even think about the past."

"Is it that Paul? Has he said something to upset you?"

"No. I mean, not directly." Ginny bit her bottom lip. This was all going horribly wrong and if she didn't fix it soon, Madelaine was going to start watching her like a hawk. "Paul's parents died in an accident when he was a kid. He got split from his sister, Kathy, in the foster care system, and he never saw her again. He looked so sad when he told me about her. I guess it just got me to thinking."

"That poor boy," Madelaine said, her expression full of sympathy. "He had his entire world yanked out from under him. No wonder you were bothered."

"Please don't tell him I said anything. I get the impression he doesn't talk about it much, and I don't want him to think I betrayed a confidence."

"Of course not." Madelaine shook her head. "That was a horrible, horrible thing to happen to a young boy." She stopped kneading the dough and looked directly at Ginny. "I promise you that if I ever have any idea how we can find something out about your past, I'll tell you. If you want, we could hire a detective and have him look into it. There's not much to go on, but I have some savings—"

Ginny sniffed, touched as always by the size of her mother's heart. "No. I'm fine, I promise. If I'm meant to find out about the past, I will."

"You sure?" Her mother didn't look convinced.

"I'm positive," Ginny said. She walked over to her mother and gave her a hug. "Have I told you lately that you're the best mom ever?"

Madelaine gave her a squeeze. "Tell me that when

I've got you measuring those windows for new curtains."

Ginny laughed as the tension between her and Madelaine dissipated. She was going to have to be very careful. Not only was Johnson's Bayou a small town full of bored, nosy people, but Madelaine was very perceptive and could easily read people.

Most especially Ginny.

A thought flashed through Ginny's mind and she remembered the blue gingham fabric that she'd found in the nightstand in the girls' home. "Mom, where did you get those old curtains, anyway? We've never had napkins to match, although you've always talked about it."

Madelaine didn't answer for a moment, and Ginny already knew what she was going to say before the words came out. "I bought them from the girls at that school," Madelaine said, her expression sad. "Some of them were quite good at sewing, and they sold stuff to some people in town for spending money—usually to buy a root beer float at the general store. They were supposed to do the napkins, when..."

Madelaine reached into a canister of flour and spread a bit more on her dough. "I just didn't have the heart to get someone else to finish the work after."

PAUL SAT IN HIS TRUCK down the street from the café on a dimly lit side street counting the minutes until 6:00 a.m. He'd tossed and turned all night on the couch, worried about too many unknowns, and knew that he needed a strong cup of coffee to get his mind back in gear—possibly an entire pot to keep it there. He scrunched down in the cab as a car turned onto Main

Street and passed. If someone noticed him sitting in the truck at this hour, it might raise questions.

As he straightened back into an upright position, he glanced at the floorboard and caught a glimpse of something on the passenger's side. The book! He'd completely forgotten that Ginny had left the book in his truck. He leaned over and picked it up from the floorboard and began to flip through the pages. He froze when he got to the page with the drawing.

Ginny was right. It was the exact same design, drawn in pencil on the page of the book.

He went back to the front of the book and turned each page slowly, scanning every square inch for any other markings, anything to indicate the book's reader, but the rest of the book was blank. Still, it was a valuable find. It was the closest he'd come to a clue about his sister in all the years he'd searched.

The sun tipped over the horizon and a warm glow began to light the quaint downtown area. The door to the hotel opened, and two couples walked out and across the road to the café. Paul glanced at his watch and was relieved to see it was almost six. He needed to take a trip to New Orleans to investigate a lead on the girl who was taken to the hospital, but he had to talk to Ginny first.

He started his truck and pulled onto Main Street then parked in front of the café. Ginny was already hustling coffee to the couples who'd entered before him, but she gave him a shy smile as he slid into a booth in the back of the café away from the other patrons. She passed menus to the couples, then looked at him and pointed to the coffeepot on the bar. He nodded and she poured a cup and made her way over.

"Was the book still there?" she asked anxiously as she placed his coffee on the table.

"Yes, and I found the drawings."

Ginny's relief was obvious. "Are you going to try and get fingerprints?"

"Yeah. I need to make a trip to New Orleans today. I'll drop the book off with my partner for him to handle."

Ginny frowned. "Does your trip have anything to do with me? No secrets, remember?"

"Not with you directly. My partner found a lead on the one girl who made it out of the school alive but it went cold after the hospital in New Orleans. I'm going to try to track down some of the hospital employees from back then and see if they can give me anything else."

"Do you think she might be your sister?"

"Maybe, but it's a slim possibility that she'd be the only one to make it out of the house that night. And I don't even know if that girl is still alive, but I have to try."

"Of course."

"I will be back tonight. In the meantime, I want you to make sure you're not alone. The festival will take care of most of the day, but if I haven't made it back here before it's over, I don't want you staying in your apartment by yourself. Have dinner with your mother, preferably in a public place."

Ginny bit her lower lip. "You think he'll come after me again?"

"I don't want to take the chance."

Ginny glanced back at the kitchen door. "Is my mom in any danger?"

"I don't think so. As long as you don't tell her anything, her behavior will be the same as always. The shooter will be watching her for a change, just like he did you. When he doesn't see one in Madelaine, he'll assume you're keeping secrets, at least for now."

Ginny's worried expression relaxed a bit. She tore a piece of paper off her order tab and wrote a number on it. "This is my cell phone. Call or text when you have an idea what time you'll be back. That way I'll know how long to stall."

Paul folded the paper and slipped it into his wallet. Before Ginny could walk away, he placed his hand on her arm. "Be careful, Ginny. Pay attention to everything around you if you can, but try not to look worried. Whoever chased us last night will be watching you. You may be able to catch him at it."

PAUL CAUGHT THE HEAD NURSE just as she was leaving the hospital. He'd spent the past four hours combing the place for anyone who worked at the hospital when the girl was a resident, and so far this was the only person he'd managed to find. The nurse stopped in the middle of the parking lot when he called her name, but judging by the look on her face, she was not thrilled with the interruption.

"I just pulled a double," she said. "Unless someone's dying, I don't want to hear about it."

"I don't work at the hospital," Paul said. "And I promise I won't take up much of your time. I'm trying to locate a patient you may have cared for."

"Patient records are confidential."

"I know, but I'm not asking about her medical condition."

The nurse frowned. "How do you know I took care of this patient?"

"I don't, but you're the only nurse left that worked here sixteen years ago."

Her eyes widened. "Sixteen years. Heavens, I can't remember who I cared for last week. Do you know how many people come through the ICU?"

"A lot, I'm sure, but this one was a little girl, about ten years old. She was pulled from a fire at a school in Johnson's Bayou."

The nurse stared over Paul's shoulder, her brow scrunched in concentration. "I think I remember something about that. No identification, right? And no one came to claim her?"

"Yes! That's the one. Did you care for her?"

"No. I didn't work the ICU then, but I remember another nurse talking about it in the break room. It was such a sad story, I guess it stuck with me." She narrowed her eyes at Paul. "What's your interest in this? She looking to sue after all these years? Everyone who doesn't want to work is looking to sue."

"Nothing like that." Paul raised one hand as the nurse gave him a skeptical look. "I swear. I'm not a lawyer and don't even like them much."

"Then what's your interest?"

"I…I think she may be my sister. Our parents died and we were separated by the foster care system. Then she disappeared. I've looked for her all these years, and this is the best lead I have…"

"Oh, my." The nurse's expression became instantly sympathetic. "But you don't have any evidence to get a court order for the records, right?"

"No."

She stared at Paul for a couple of seconds, and he could tell some sort of mental war was going on inside of her. Finally, she pulled a slip of paper from her purse and wrote a name on it. "That was the nurse I heard talking in the break room. She retired several years ago, but if she's alive, she may be able to tell you something."

Paul curled his hand around the paper. "Thank you! You don't know how much I appreciate this."

The nurse nodded and gave him a quick hug. "I hope you find your sister."

It took his partner an agonizing thirty minutes to find an address for the name the nurse had given him, and he was further dismayed to find that the woman no longer lived in the New Orleans area but had retired to a small community about two hours away. He checked his watch and was surprised to realize it was already two o'clock in the afternoon and he'd completely skipped lunch.

As he stared out the windshield of his car, a silent debate ran in his mind. If he visited the woman today, he wouldn't get back to Johnson's Bayou until nighttime. He wasn't as concerned about Ginny during the day at the café and the festival, but he worried about her at night. But if the woman had answers…

Finally, he pressed Ginny's cell phone number into his phone. She answered after a couple of rings and he could hear the noise from the festival in the background.

"How's it going there?" he asked.

"It's busy. I'm almost sold out of my jewelry."

"Have you noticed anything suspicious?"

"No, and I've been watching. I mean, not obviously

so, but I've been on alert. I haven't seen anyone paying attention to me except for buyers."

"Any locals stop by and ask you questions?"

Ginny laughed. "*Every* local stopped by and they all asked questions, but nothing outside of the norm, given that everyone seems to know I had dinner with a handsome stranger last night. What about you? Did you have any luck tracking down the other girl?"

"I have a lead on a nurse who might have cared for the girl when she was in ICU."

"Oh, that's really good!"

"Yeah, the only problem is, she retired to a small town about two hours from New Orleans. If I go there today, I won't make it back to Johnson's Bayou until tonight. I don't want you alone, especially after dark."

"Don't worry about me. I'll have dinner in town with my mom, and if you're still not back by the time we finish, I'll go visit her at her house for a while. She's been harping on me to help her hang some pictures for weeks now."

It sounded perfect, but Paul still felt that niggle of fear in the pit of his stomach. "Promise me that if your mother can't do dinner or contracts malaria and doesn't want to hang the pictures that you won't stay at your apartment by yourself."

"I promise, but it's pointless. Madelaine would have dinner and hang those pictures even if she had one foot in the grave. You don't know her well."

"Okay. Keep watch and make note of anything odd. I'll call you as soon as I'm leaving the nurse's house so that you know what time to expect me back in Johnson's Bayou."

He made the drive in a little under two hours, but

it felt like ten. He spent the time alternating between wondering if the woman would have the answers he'd been looking for and worrying about leaving Ginny alone. By the time he pulled up in front of her house, he had to take a minute to regain control of his emotions.

Finally, he stepped out of his car and approached the house, praying that she was home. His partner had been unsuccessful locating a home or cell number, so he hadn't been able to call ahead. It would be just his luck if the woman was on a monthlong tour of Europe. He rang the doorbell, and his pulse quickened when a dog began to bark inside. A couple of seconds later, an older, Creole woman opened the door.

"Mrs. LeDoux?" he asked.

"Yes."

"My name is Paul Stanton and I was hoping you would talk to me about a patient you may have cared for sixteen years ago at New Orleans General."

The woman frowned. "I don't talk about patients. That wouldn't be right."

"I understand, but in this case, you may change your mind." Paul explained briefly why he was looking for his sister and why he felt she may be able to help him.

"I remember the case. It was so sad. Probably why it's stuck in my mind." She opened the door and waved him inside. "Might as well come in before my tea gets cold."

Paul stepped inside and followed the woman into the kitchen, where she served them both a cup of hot tea. "Thank you for talking to me," Paul said as he took a sip of tea. "I've been looking for so long, and even though it's a long shot, I have to follow this to the end, just to be sure."

"Certainly. I remember the night they brought the girl into the hospital. Came by helicopter, which always signals something dire. She was such a pretty little thing."

"Can you tell me what she looked like?"

"She was a white girl—wavy brown hair, brown eyes, maybe ten years old. Skinny, but not malnourished. Just one of those active builds, I guess you'd call it."

Paul nodded. The description fit his sister perfectly. And probably a million other kids, but at least it wasn't the end of the line for him yet. "How badly was she injured?"

"At first, she was in and out of consciousness, but the pain finally won out and her body gave up. She slipped into a coma and stayed that way for almost a year. The doctors had no idea why, as her injuries had long since healed and all her vital signs appeared normal. She just wouldn't wake up."

"But she finally did?"

"It was the strangest thing ever. One day, she just sat up in bed and rang the nurse to ask for an ice-cream cone, of all things."

Paul's pulse quickened. His sister's favorite treat was an ice-cream cone. "Did she remember anything?"

"Not a thing. The police had been so hopeful when she awakened, but it's like her life before waking up in the hospital had been scrubbed clean out of her mind."

"So what happened to her after that?"

The woman shook her head. "I'm not sure, really. They moved her to a room in the regular wing, which wasn't my area. I know she did physical therapy for a while because of the lack of use of her muscles, but I don't know what happened to her after that. I suppose given that no one came to claim her, and since she didn't know who she was, that she was placed with a family."

Paul tried to control his disappointment, but he was certain it showed on his face.

She sighed. "I'm sorry I can't help you any more than that."

"Don't be sorry," he reassured her. "At least I know she left the hospital alive. That gives me hope that if it is my sister, she's still alive today. It could have been the end of the line."

"I suppose you're right, but it seems like small comfort."

Paul rose from the table and thanked the woman for her time. As he walked out the door, he found himself thinking that he couldn't agree more. It was small comfort, but comfort nonetheless.

THE NURSE WATCHED PAUL through the slats in the window blinds as he got into his car and pulled away. When the man had first approached her years ago, she'd thought him a bit suspicious-minded. He'd told her the real story behind the girl's past—that she'd been placed in the school by the foster care system to hide her from an abusive father. The man figured if she didn't remember, that was for the best. Then there was no way her father could find her. As the years went by, no one ever asked about the girl, but he continued to make the annual payments. Finally she decided it was full-blown paranoia, but if the man wanted to waste money that way, she wasn't going to tell him anything different. After all, she'd kept her end of the bargain.

And now, after all the years, the visit the man had been expecting had occurred.

It took her a while to find the man's phone number, buried deep in her desk behind years of paperwork, but finally she located the yellowed piece of paper. She pulled out the prepaid cell phone—the only form of communication she bothered to keep these days— and dialed. He answered immediately.

"It's Nurse Agnes," she said, using the name they'd agreed on long ago.

"Has something happened?" The anxiety in the man's voice was apparent.

"A man came to visit me asking about the girl. Claimed he was looking for his sister, as they were separated as kids by the foster care system. It was a good story and he delivered it well. If you hadn't warned me someone might come asking, I would have believed his story."

"You didn't tell him anything?"

"Only what we agreed upon." She hesitated for a moment, a question hovering on the tip of her tongue. It was none of her business and the man wouldn't like her asking, but something inside her had to know. "You're going to keep her safe, right?"

Her query was met with complete silence.

"Look," she said, "I know you don't give details, and that's fine. I just want to know that you're not going to allow her abuser to find her. He probably hired that man. I want to know that she's safe."

"She's safe."

The man disconnected the call and the nurse placed

her cell phone on the desk. The man had promised he'd protect the girl. He'd paid her all these years to keep her hidden from the man who'd abused her—her own father.

But something didn't feel right.

A flash of Paul's face as he told her his story passed through her mind. He was so earnest, so passionate and seemed so sincere. Had she really grown so old and unaware that he'd charmed her into believing his story?

Or was he telling the truth?

THE MAN CLOSED HIS cell phone and stared across the town square at Ginny. He wondered if she knew why the man she'd been seeing had come to Johnson's Bayou. If what he'd told the nurse was the truth, then it was no coincidence that he'd hooked up with Ginny almost immediately after arriving in town. But had he told her why? Or was he just hoping she'd give him information?

Clearly, the lying "vacationer" had decided Ginny wasn't the woman he sought, or he wouldn't have tracked down the nurse. The nurse hadn't told him anything important, but the whole situation didn't sit well with the man. He'd kept the LeBlanc School secrets for a lot of years, managing to hide everything from the police and others who came behind them.

If the detective succeeded in blowing the lid off the past, the fallout was bound to come home to roost. Two more years and he was set to retire. Was set to leave Johnson's Bayou and never have to think about the past.

Now he had to do something about the vacationer, or that would never happen.

Chapter Nine

Ginny placed the few items left on her table in the storage container and closed the top. Madelaine was supposed to meet her at her booth at closing time, but aside from a brief wave when she went by earlier chasing after a couple of her best friend's grandchildren, Ginny hadn't seen her mother since they closed the café that morning.

She glanced west at the sinking sun and checked her cell phone for the hundredth time that afternoon. No messages. She wondered if Paul had found the nurse and if he'd gotten information. With any luck, no message meant he was still chasing down leads and that he'd find something useful.

She grabbed her storage container and started across the town square. In the meantime, she needed to activate plan B—find Madelaine and invite her to dinner. Then attempt to act normal while the entire time, she'd be wondering what Paul was doing and what he'd discovered. She'd made it to the edge of the square when she heard Madelaine calling her.

She turned as Madelaine hurried across the square, huffing as she propelled her slightly overweight frame at a speed it normally didn't obtain. "Thought I was going to miss you," Madelaine wheezed as she leaned over to catch her breath.

"You're just in time."

"Got caught watching those grandkids of Carol's while she tried some newfangled skin care line one of the New Orleans sellers was hawking. Lord, those kids can move. I've run more this afternoon than I have in the last ten years."

"Running is at a premium in the café unless people start wanting to wear their coffee," Ginny teased.

Madelaine straightened up and laughed. "You'd probably be better than me. You're still in shape and always had good balance. How were sales today?"

"I only have three pieces left, total. I'm glad I made more than I thought I'd need."

"That's great! So…are you meeting your sexy new man for dinner?"

Ginny felt a blush creep up her neck. "He's not *my* man. And no, he had some business in New Orleans today and didn't know when he'd return."

Madelaine shook her head. "Conducting business on vacation. Not a good sign. The last thing you want is a workaholic, no matter how good-looking and charming he may be."

"I'm sure it was important for him to interrupt his vacation time. But anyway, that means I'm officially free tonight, so I thought I'd see if you wanted to have dinner at Maude's—my treat."

"Look at you, Miss Moneybags." Madelaine smiled. "Sell a little jewelry and suddenly you're Donald Trump. Well, as much as I'd love to get home and remove this bra and shoes, I'd like someone to cook for me and clean it up even more."

"Then dinner it is," Ginny said, relieved that she wasn't going to have to do any odd maneuvering to convince Madelaine to have dinner with her. She already felt out of sorts, and it was going to be hard to keep that from her intuitive mother. Cajoling her into dinner if she'd said no would have immediately sent up alarms.

"I want to drop this off at the café, then we can go eat."

"Might be a bit of a wait," Madelaine warned. "All the visitors got to leave the festival before you, and since it's the only place in town to eat at night, I imagine they're going to be doing a booming business."

"We could always keep summer hours at the café and give people another alternative," Ginny suggested, already knowing what her mother would say.

"No way! I count the days every year till the festival, when we change to breakfast and lunch only. I like my evenings off."

Ginny smiled. "Well, I'm in no hurry. Besides, it will probably be worth the wait. I heard they put peach cobbler on the menu for tonight."

"Peach cobbler! You were holding back on me." Madelaine tugged on her arm as she began to walk faster. "Let's get a move on. I don't want them running out."

MADELAINE LEANED BACK in the restaurant chair and sighed. "I haven't eaten that much in years, but I just couldn't help it. Maude really outdid herself. Homemade chicken and dumplings and peach cobbler. She must have been up cooking all night."

Ginny forced herself to put her fork down before

she exploded. "I know. I don't think I'll eat again for a week." She pushed back her chair and rose. "Ask Amy for the bill when she comes by again. I'll be back in a sec."

She tried to appear nonchalant as she made her way across the restaurant to the ladies' room, but every time someone stopped her to chat, she wanted to scream. Just minutes before, she could swear she'd heard her phone signal that she'd received a text message. It had been almost two hours since she'd texted Paul to let him know she was having dinner with Madelaine, and she'd yet to hear a word out of him.

Reaching into her jeans pocket, she pulled out her cell phone and checked the display. "On my way" the message read. She struggled to contain her disappointment that he hadn't said anything about his investigation, then pressed in his number. Might as well call and ask.

The call went straight to voice mail. Darn. She checked the time on Paul's message and saw it had arrived a little over an hour ago. He was probably on one of the lonely stretches of highway where cell phone signal faded in and out, and likely still two hours or more from Johnson's Bayou.

It looked as if she was going to have to hang pictures with Madelaine for a while in order to keep her promise of not being alone. If she'd known for sure Paul wasn't going to return in time for her to avoid the manual-labor portion of the night, she wouldn't have eaten as much. All that sugar had her wishing for her bed, not a project with her mother.

She accessed text messaging and sent a message to Paul.

Going to mom's. Call when you arrive.

As soon as Paul drove into an area with coverage, he'd receive the message. There was nothing else to do now but wait, and wonder and worry, and help her mom hang pictures. Sighing, she left the restroom and pulled out her wallet as she walked back to the table.

"Do you still need me to help hang those pictures you bought?" Ginny asked as she laid some bills on the table.

Madelaine brightened and rose from her chair. "Yes. In fact, I picked up two more pictures at the festival. I think I have enough to finish the dining room."

"Great. The one room in the house you never use will be the best decorated," Ginny teased.

An hour later, Ginny wished she had volunteered for something other than picture hanging, like scrubbing the bathroom or mowing the lawn in the dark. Madelaine refused to eyeball the pictures as she usually did, and instead insisted that they measure the wall and do calculations to get everything perfectly balanced.

When the house phone rang, Ginny dropped the tape measure on the table, relieved to have a break. A couple of minutes later, Madelaine hurried back into the dining room, carrying her purse and wearing a worried expression. "Carol slipped and fell in the shower. The paramedics want to take her to the hospital in New Orleans to have her head looked at, but Carol's keeping those grandkids and can't reach her daughter. I'm going to run over there and watch them until their parents pick them up."

Ginny felt a momentary twinge of panic when she realized Madelaine was leaving her alone, but it would have been completely out of character to ask to tag along. Ginny wasn't overly comfortable around Carol's grandkids, who relished in practical jokes. It wouldn't surprise her in the least to find they were behind Carol's fall.

"I'm sorry to take off on you," Madelaine said as she pulled her car keys from her purse. "I'll probably be gone an hour. We can work on this another night."

"No. That's okay. I can finish it up myself. We've already marked the wall, so it's just a matter of hanging the brackets and the pictures." She gave her mom a hug. "Give Carol my best."

"If you're gone when I return, I'll see you tomorrow morning," Madelaine said as she rushed out the door.

Ginny hurried to lock the door and peeked out the window into the darkness. For a moment, she thought she saw light flickering in the swamp, but she blinked and it was gone. It hadn't been a beam of light, as from a flashlight, but rather had danced like fire. But fire couldn't have disappeared so quickly.

Great. Now, she was imagining things. She thought about leaving her mother's house, but she had no idea where she would go. Maude's was closed for the night, and the hotel gave customers passkeys to the front door rather than covering the cost of staffing at night. There wasn't a single convenience store anywhere in town, and the last place that was safe was her apartment.

She took a deep breath and blew it out. There was no reason to assume she was in any danger. She'd watched carefully all day and at dinner and hadn't noticed anything out of the ordinary. Hadn't had a single feeling that something was off. But her mother's house was close to the swamp and a good ten acres from the nearest neighbor and all that was spooking her.

She walked back into the dining room and picked up the drill and the first picture bracket. By the time she finished hanging all the pictures, Paul would be there or her mother would be back. An hour at the most. And if she kept busy, it would fly by. Besides, Madelaine would be thrilled when she returned home and saw all the pictures hanging in perfect balance on her dining room wall.

Positioning the first screw on the mark, she placed the drill against it and began to screw it into the drywall. She finished the first screw, then started on the second, but when it was halfway in, she released the trigger on the drill and froze. There it was—the almost imperceptible sound of a foot stepping on dead leaves.

She placed the drill on the table and crept over to the window to peek outside. The front porch light reached only twenty feet or so into the yard, leaving the surrounding area black. She strained to make out movement, to hear the same noise again, but she couldn't see a thing.

But she knew he was there.

Somewhere out in the darkness, someone was watching. She could feel his eyes on the house, on her—almost as if he could see straight through the walls. Her hands trembled as she pulled her cell phone from her pocket and checked the display. Nothing. She pressed redial for Paul's number and cursed when it went straight to voice mail again.

Think. You have to think.

She could call the sheriff, but what would she say— that she had a feeling someone was watching her? Given her past, anything she said that was remotely out of the ordinary would be subject to scrutiny. And even if the sheriff came, Ginny knew he wouldn't find anything to support her suspicions.

Calling her mother wasn't an option, because that would put her in the line of fire. She hurried down the hall into the kitchen and removed a butcher knife from the block on the counter. Edging the curtains on the kitchen window to the side, she estimated the distance between the back door and her car. Probably twenty feet, give or take. If she could make it to her car, she could drive to the sheriff's office and sit with the dispatcher.

To hell with them if they thought she was crazy. At least she'd be alive.

She retrieved her purse and car keys from the kitchen counter and eased up to the back door. And that's when she heard the crack of a single branch out back. She sucked in a breath so hard her chest ached. Her pulse quickened as she edged the curtain on the kitchen window to the side and tried to see outside. The back porch light illuminated a small area of the backyard, but someone could easily be hiding behind her car or the storage shed.

The only sound was the clock that ticked on the kitchen wall, seeming to mark every heartbeat. Squinting, she scanned back and forth from the house to the swamp behind it. Nothing moved. Nothing made a sound. But she knew he was there.

The floor creaked behind her and as she spun around, something hard slammed into the side of her head, knocking her back into the kitchen cabinet and down onto the floor. Her vision blurred for a moment as she scrambled up from the floor and saw a masked figure in front of her. During her fall, she'd dropped the knife, and it was on the floor between her and the intruder.

She lunged for the knife as the intruder sprang. Wrapping her hand around the hilt, she drove it into the intruder's leg. He cried out as she skirted around him and ran out the back door. She pulled her car keys from her pocket and fumbled with them, dropping them onto the ground.

The kitchen door slammed behind her and she fought back complete panic as she scrambled to retrieve the keys and press the remote to open the door. She jumped into the car and tried to slam the door, but he grabbed it. She saw the flash of the butcher knife in his hand, the shiny metal marred with blood.

She pulled the door with one hand and shoved the intruder with the other, but he was too strong. Struggling to hold the door partially closed with one hand, she started the car with her other, put it in drive and floored the accelerator. The intruder clung to the door for a moment, trying to jump into the car, but the bumpy lawn was too much and he finally let go.

Ginny wheeled the car around in the backyard and headed for the road, scanning her mirrors for the intruder. Did he have a vehicle somewhere close? Was he going to come after her? She steered her car onto the road, spraying gravel as the car slid sideways. Clenching the steering wheel, she focused on the road and fought to maintain control of the car without lessening her speed.

A flash of light caught her eye and she glanced in the rearview mirror. Her heart fell when she saw the single headlight of an ATV about a hundred yards behind her and quickly closing the gap. Her cell phone rang and she gripped the steering wheel tighter with her left hand and pulled the cell phone out of her jeans pocket with her right.

Paul!

She pressed the answer button and shouted, "He's after me, trying to kill me."

"Where are you?"

"Landry Road—my mother's house. He's on an ATV—"

The bend in the road was in front of her before she could even register that she'd come that far. She dropped the phone as she slammed on the brakes and grabbed the steering wheel with both hands, yanking it to the left to make the turn. The car lost traction on the loose gravel and began to slide. She released the brake and prayed that the car would regain some grip on the road, but a second later, it slid off the road and into the ditch, slamming against the embankment.

The last thing she saw before she lost consciousness was the single headlight of the ATV closing in behind her.

Chapter Ten

"Damn it!" Paul heard the crash through the cell phone before the call dropped completely.

The tires on Paul's truck squealed as he made a hard turn from the paved road onto the gravel top of Landry Road. Thank goodness he'd researched everything on Ginny and knew exactly where her mother lived. Otherwise, he wouldn't have known where to go. Every second counted, and he was already afraid he was going to be too late.

He should never have left her alone. He could have waited until tomorrow to talk to the nurse. His impatience might have cost Ginny her life. Switching his headlights to bright, he drove as fast as he could maneuver on the pitch-black, winding road. The gravel made speed challenging, and the last thing he wanted to do was have a wreck.

He was almost on top of Ginny's car before he saw it in the ditch. He slammed on his brakes and the truck slid a good fifty feet before finally coming to a halt. He jumped out of the truck and ran for the car just as a gunshot sounded. The bullet whizzed past his ear and he dove in the ditch, pulling out his pistol as he rolled.

He scrambled up and peered over the edge of the

ditch, able to make out the outline of the ATV just beyond the reach of his truck's headlights. Lowering his pistol over the embankment, he took aim at the ATV and squeezed off a couple of rounds. He heard the pinging of a bullet hitting metal and a couple of seconds later, the ATV engine roared to life. Gravel crunched as the ATV took off, and Paul wondered which direction the rider was going.

He held his position for a couple of seconds, but as the sound of the engine began to fade, he knew the killer was fleeing. Shoving his pistol in his waistband, he ran to the car, yanked the car door open and pushed the air bag to the side. Ginny was slumped over the steering wheel, and his heart pounded in his chest as he placed his finger on her neck. Relief coursed through him when he felt her pulse, clear and strong.

He gave Ginny a cursory inspection to make sure there were no compound fractures, then scooped her up and carried her to his truck, gently placing her on the front seat. He knew he shouldn't move her, but calling for an ambulance gave the ATV driver time to return or worse, sneak up on them through the swamp as they waited.

He'd take his chances.

There was an emergency medical center just outside of Johnson's Bayou that served several nearby towns. It wasn't as good as a hospital in New Orleans, but she'd be safe, and if needed they could transport her to the city by helicopter. He pulled the phone from his pocket and called the center so that they'd be ready for his arrival.

Glancing down at Ginny's pale expression and inert body, he said a silent prayer that she would be okay.

GINNY LOOKED UP AT Sheriff Blackwell from her bed at the emergency clinic. He stared down at her, frowning as he finished taking notes on her story.

"Can you give me a description?" Sheriff Blackwell asked.

"No. He was wearing a mask, in navy knit. It looked homemade."

"Eye color?"

"I didn't get close enough to see," Ginny said, frustrated that she could provide so little information.

"Did he touch anything besides the knife and the door?"

"I don't think so, but it wouldn't matter anyway. He was wearing leather gloves."

"And you have no idea how he got into the house?"

"No. I heard the noise outside, but I had no idea he'd gotten inside until he was right behind me." She crossed her arms over her chest and shivered at the memory.

Sheriff Blackwell blew out a breath, clearly as frustrated with the situation as Ginny. "I am really sorry this happened to you. I imagine it took a couple years off your life and your mother's. One of my deputies is working the house now for forensic evidence."

The sheriff turned his attention to Paul. "How is it you came to rescue Ginny?"

"I was on my way back from New Orleans and called her as she was fleeing the house. She managed to tell me where she was and that she was being pursued before she crashed. I had just pulled into Johnson's Bayou and was close to the turnoff for her mother's place, so I drove as fast as I could over there."

The sheriff studied Paul while he told his story and

stared at him for a couple of seconds when he'd finished. He must have decided it sounded reasonable,
because he finally nodded and continued questioning
him. "You said the car was at the ninety-degree bend
in the road, right? Where was the other guy?"

"He was up the road about forty feet, off to the
north side. He shot at me as soon as I got out of the
truck. I jumped into the ditch and fired back over the
embankment."

Sheriff Blackwell narrowed his eyes at Paul. "You
always run around with a pistol in your waistband?"

"I do when I call someone and they tell me someone's after them. Otherwise, it's locked in my glove
box. I have my permit."

Sheriff Blackwell waved a hand in dismissal.
"You're not the one in question here. Besides, half the
people in the parish carry guns." The sheriff blew out a
breath. "I gotta tell you, there's not a lot to go on here.
Unless the deputy comes up with something at your
mom's house, there's not going to be a lot I can do by
way of investigating."

"One of my shots hit metal," Paul said. "You can
identify the ATV by the bullet hole. How many people
in Johnson's Bayou own ATVs?" Paul asked.

"Half the male population, maybe more, and a good
portion of females. Besides, I've gotten four reports
of stolen ATVs today alone. Happens once or twice a
year all on the same day. A real professional job. The
ATVs are all stolen within the same twenty-four-hour
period, usually during the festival or something else
that's got the townsfolk distracted. By the time they
realize the ATVs are gone, the guy who stole them is
long gone."

"If he was only stealing ATVs, why go to my mother's house?" Ginny asked. "She doesn't own an ATV."

The sheriff shook his head. "I don't know. Maybe he knew Madelaine owned the café and thought she kept cash in the house. He might have thought it was an easy score."

"Mom would never keep cash from the café in her house. She drops it off at the bank lockbox every day."

"You and I know that, but someone who doesn't know Madelaine wouldn't. Like I said, they may have just been looking for an easy score."

"I stabbed him," Ginny reminded the sheriff. "He took the knife, but there should be blood on the kitchen floor. You can check it, right?"

"I'm afraid not. He must have gone back to your mom's house and cleaned up. My deputy said the kitchen smelled like bleach and the floor had been scrubbed with it."

"If he wanted to clean up, why did he chase me? He could have just let me go, cleaned up the kitchen and waltzed right back out of town, if he's really the professional you think he is."

A bit of red crept up Sheriff Blackwell's neck. "Now, look here—I'm not saying for certain what happened. I'm just telling you the most logical conclusion based on years of doing this job. Maybe he thought you'd be able to recognize him. Maybe he panicked. You've got it in your mind that he was trying to kill you, but I'm guessing a male criminal may have taken a good look at you and gotten another idea."

Ginny sucked in a breath so hard her chest hurt. Her mind hadn't even gone there, and she wished the sheriff hadn't taken it there, either. Paul squeezed her hand and she glanced up at him. He gave her a barely imperceptible shake of his head and she knew he was telling her to let it go. This avenue with the sheriff was a dead end.

She was deliberating whether or not to lay everything out to Sheriff Blackwell regardless of Paul's obvious reticence when Madelaine came back into the room, removing that option altogether. She wasn't about to have her mother any more worried than she already was.

"They don't think you need to go to the hospital in New Orleans," Madelaine said, frowning, "but they want you to stay overnight for observation."

"No," Ginny said. "I'm fine except for a bit of a headache. I'll stay for a couple of hours, but then I'm going home. I've got a busy day tomorrow, and don't even start arguing with me about taking the day off. The café will be packed with everyone leaving town now that the festival's over, and a couple of shop owners from New Orleans said they're stopping by in the morning to talk to me about my jewelry."

Madelaine started to argue, but the sheriff, likely sensing a never-ending family squabble, interrupted. "I know your heart's here with your daughter, Madelaine, but I'd really like it if you'd come with me to your house. I need to know if anything's missing and see if we can figure out how he got in. The sooner I have the facts, the faster I can get out an alert to other towns for this guy."

"I'm not leaving her alone," Madelaine said.

"I'll stay with her," Paul said. "I can't help the sheriff with your house, but you can. Please go. I promise I won't leave her side."

Madelaine was clearly torn between wanting to mother Ginny and wanting to contribute to capturing the man who'd hurt her. She looked back and forth between Ginny, Paul and Sheriff Blackwell and finally grabbed her purse from the chair she'd tossed it in earlier and gave Ginny a kiss.

"Call me if you need anything," Madelaine said, then turned to Paul. "And if her condition gets worse, *make* her go to the hospital in New Orleans. I mean it—or you'll both need medical attention."

"If the doctors say she needs to go, I'll make her go," Paul promised.

Madelaine didn't look completely convinced, but she walked to the door and looked over at the sheriff. "Better get a move on. If one of those silly deputies of yours makes a mess in my house, you're going to hear about it for a year."

Sheriff Blackwell, wearing the expression of a much-maligned and abused male, followed Madelaine out of the room, smart enough to keep silent.

"Do you think it happened like the sheriff said?" Ginny demanded as soon as everyone had cleared the room.

"I think it's possible, but very unlikely, given the circumstances." Paul removed an extra pillow from a shelf in the corner and motioned to Ginny to lean forward so he could place it behind her. "But you have to remember, you and I are the only people aware of those circumstances, and the sheriff isn't going to put any stock in a 'feeling.' We need evidence."

Ginny leaned back on the plump pillow but was far too wound up to relax. "He tried to kill me. How much more evidence do we need?"

"Evidence that it was personal and not some random attack associated with stealing four-wheelers. I know it's hard to be objective given what we know, but put yourself in his shoes. Even if we told him everything we knew, what reason does he have for thinking someone's after you?"

"Someone was in my apartment."

"With no sign of forced entry."

"He shot at us when we were at the school."

"He could have been a poacher either mistaking us for deer or trying to prevent anyone from talking about his poaching."

Ginny sighed. "You're right. There's a logical assumption he could make about every incident, but isn't it an enormous coincidence that all of them are happening to the same person within a matter of days? Especially someone like me. I've never been in trouble and don't have any enemies."

"That's not true," Paul said quietly. "You just aren't aware of who your enemies are."

Ginny was silent for a moment. Paul was right, but that didn't mean she had to like it. In fact, now that she'd moved past fear for her life and fear that she'd sustained a serious injury, she was moving straight toward mad.

Paul shook his head, clearly frustrated. "Even tonight is questionable. If he really wanted to kill you, why not shoot you? He had a gun. Why sneak up behind you and crack you over the head?"

Ginny stared at Paul and drummed her fingers on the blanket. "I hadn't even thought of that. Then what in the world did he want? It doesn't make sense. Unless it's like the sheriff suggested…"

Paul frowned. "As distasteful as the thought is, it's not impossible. But I still don't think that's the answer. I have no concrete reason for thinking this, but I still believe that it's all connected to your past. We just don't have enough information to connect the pieces."

"Since there's no evidence, what do we do about tonight—nothing?" she asked. "Because, I've got to tell you, that's not good enough for me."

"Me, either," Paul agreed. "The first thing we do is figure out as much as we can about your attacker."

"I told the sheriff everything I knew."

"Actually, you probably didn't. But given his view on things, I didn't see the point in attempting to draw more information out of you while he was here."

Ginny stared at Paul, her interest piqued. "What kind of information?"

"Let's start with a physical description. How tall was he?"

"I don't know. I was too panicked."

Paul sat on the bed next to her and placed his hand on her arm. "Take a deep breath and close your eyes. Now, picture that scene you described in the kitchen— you were on the floor, looking up at the attacker. How much space was in between the attacker's head and the ceiling?"

The scene replayed in Ginny's mind as if she were watching a movie. She felt her heart quicken, but she managed to focus on what Paul asked for. "About two feet," she said, surprising herself that the answer had been gained so easily.

"And how high are the ceilings in your mom's house?"

"Eight feet."

"Good. So now we know he's approximately six feet tall."

Ginny nodded, starting to feel a little hope. "That's great! Can we do more?"

"When you stabbed him, what part of the leg did you hit him in?"

"Just above the knee. I remember thinking I was lucky I didn't hit the kneecap or it wouldn't have gone in." She covered her mouth with her hands. "I can't believe I thought all that or remembered it."

"That's great," Paul said, his voice encouraging. "Now, how high off the floor was your hand when you stabbed him?"

Ginny sat completely upright in bed and held her arm down off the side of the bed, trying to replay the scene in her mind. "Maybe this high," she said, holding her hands apart to show Paul the estimated distance.

Paul smiled. "So now we know that he's approximately six feet tall and has long legs. Now, let's talk about weight—trim or loose?"

"Not skinny or fat. Broad shoulders and some size, but more like man-size versus boy-size, not fat. Does that make any sense?"

"He was a mature man. That makes complete sense. Now, think about his movement—was he fast, agile?"

"He sprang at me at the same time I went for the knife. We were probably covering the same distance, but I got there first. He didn't seem to have an injury or anything, but I moved faster. Does that mean he's older?"

"Possibly," Paul said. "You did really good, Ginny. I think your attacker lives in Johnson's Bayou. That stab wound is going to give him trouble, but he won't seek medical treatment for it. He'll do his best to hide it altogether, but if we're keeping a close watch, we may be able to catch someone slipping."

Ginny blew out a breath. It wasn't much, but it was more than they had before. She looked up at Paul. "I never got to thank you for rescuing me. I don't know what would have happened if you hadn't been there."

"I didn't…" Paul broke off speaking and looked at her, the care, compassion and fear still resident in his expression, along with something else that Ginny hadn't seen in a long time. Her eyes widened as he leaned closer.

She knew he was going to kiss her, but when his lips touched hers, she was still completely unprepared for the surge of emotion and desire that coursed through her.

"Excuse me." A woman's voice sounded from the doorway, and Ginny and Paul sprang apart. Ginny looked over at the young nurse.

"I'm sorry to interrupt," the nurse said shyly, "but I need to check your head. The injury, I mean."

Paul rose from the bed. "I'm going to find the doctor and see how long you need to stay."

Ginny watched him leave the room as the nurse removed the bandage from her forehead. Check her head, indeed. What in the world was she thinking, letting Paul kiss her? And even worse, kissing him back? She was going to completely ignore the fact that she'd enjoyed it.

The last thing she needed right now was another complication. Her usually uncomplicated life had just exploded on every level. Adding romantic feelings to the mix was a recipe for disaster, especially at a time when her emotions were already running so high. More complication meant more distraction—her attention spread out over too many places.

Right now, she needed to focus only on staying alive.

Chapter Eleven

Sheriff Blackwell studied the kitchen then frowned. Madelaine stood beside him, hands on her hips, wanting answers she'd bet he didn't have.

"Well?" she demanded. "How did he get in my house?"

"I don't know. When the deputy got here, the house was locked tight. He had to bust out a panel on your kitchen door to open the dead bolt. All the windows were locked tight, and you said they were all that way when you left. Unless you forgot about an open window, I have no idea. As far as I can see, there's no other way into this place, unless you can walk through walls."

"My daughter wasn't attacked by a ghost, or he wouldn't have bled on my kitchen floor."

The sheriff ran a hand through his hair, clearly frustrated. "I know that, but what do you want me to say? Does anyone else have a key besides you and Ginny?"

"No, and those locks are new from when I replaced the doors last year. Only two keys came with that lock, and Ginny and I account for both of them."

"You didn't make a spare?"

"Yes, but I keep it in my desk drawer at the café, not under the doormat like a fool."

Sheriff Blackwell looked up and down the hallway, then out the back door once more before coming to stand directly in front of Madelaine. "How's Ginny been lately?"

"What do you mean? She's been Ginny." Madelaine stared at him, wondering what in the world had gotten into the man. It was as if he'd lost all common sense. Suddenly, it hit her and she felt a flush creep up her neck and onto her face.

"I'm certain," she said, struggling to control her rising anger, "that you're not suggesting she imagined all of this."

The sheriff sighed. "Madelaine, I'm not trying to make you mad or cast any aspersions on Ginny, but you got to look at the facts. The house was locked tight when my deputies arrived and you can't do that without a key. There was no blood on the floor to substantiate her story of an attack."

Madelaine pointed to the knife holder. "My butcher knife is missing, and I don't clean my floor with bleach."

Sheriff Blackwell looked down at the floor and shuffled his feet. "It may be that Ginny took the knife herself, maybe tossed it in the swamp as she drove away. Maybe she spilled bleach on the floor earlier and doesn't remember because she spooked herself."

"And the ATV? She imagined that, too?"

"The deputies have scanned every square inch of the road and there's no sign of ATV tracks."

"So you've got a logical reason for dismissing the entire thing as imagined or misunderstood."

"I'm sorry, Madelaine. I know how hard that is to wrap your mind around, but it's something both of us have to consider."

Madelaine struggled to control her frustration. She knew what he thought. Knew what they all thought—that Ginny was a ticking time bomb and one day the past would come back to haunt them. All because Madelaine had taken her in and kept her in Johnson's Bayou. But a bunch of foolishness wasn't going to keep Madelaine from doing what she darn well pleased—not then and not now. And what pleased Madelaine was protecting her daughter.

"He could have covered his tracks," she argued. "He could have lifted a key from me or Ginny at some point and made a copy. We're not always careful with our keys when we're working."

Sheriff Blackwell nodded. "Yeah, he could have, but that's an awful lot of planning to attack someone with no provocation. Far as I know, no one in Johnson's Bayou or anywhere else has a problem with Ginny."

"Maybe it was the other thing you suggested," Madelaine said, not wanting to actually say the word. "Maybe he was fixated on my Ginny and it wasn't about stealing or killing her."

"Perhaps. But he would have had to already have a key made, already have an ATV stashed, already have bleach ready to go. That means premeditation and stalking. And on any given night, it would have been far easier to break in and attack her in her apartment, as all the businesses on that end of the street close up at night. Why wait to follow her out here?"

"I don't know," Madelaine said, her frustration hitting its peak. "You're the sheriff. You're supposed to be the one figuring this out. All I know is that my daughter is not crazy and she's not a liar. If she says someone was in here and he attacked her, then you best believe it happened. I suppose you think Paul is lying along with her?"

"No, but we have to assume Ginny was panicked when he called her. I believe he heard a shot and took a shot at someone, but likely it was poachers."

"You have an answer for everything, don't you?" She glared at him. "Well, you've got a choice—you can pretend my daughter's crazy and sit around and wait for it to happen again. But I wouldn't want to be wrong if I were you—especially when it comes around to election time."

Sheriff Blackwell drew his shoulders back and stood up straight. "If you're implying that I'm going to do anything less than my job looking into this, you're wrong. I'm just giving you an alternative in case I come back with nothing. I can't create evidence, and if I don't find anything to support Ginny's story, that's something the two of you are going to have to figure out how to deal with."

He left the kitchen and never looked back as he exited the house, closing the kitchen door behind him. Madelaine stared at the door, her mind whirling with thoughts, and none of them good. Either someone was stalking Ginny, or Ginny was imagining it all. Neither option was a good one for a mother to consider.

She glanced down at her watch. It had been two hours since she left the medical center. If she knew Ginny, that girl had already pestered Paul into taking her home. She grabbed her purse and locked the door behind her, for whatever good it might do. She wanted

Ginny to rest, but she knew better than anyone that once Ginny was rested, she'd close up like a vise. It was a low-down dirty trick to ferret information out of her daughter when she was in a weakened state, but Madelaine wasn't above using any trick necessary to be a good mother.

GINNY HAD JUST GOTTEN settled in bed with Paul hovering nearby, when there was a knock at her door. Paul looked at her with raised eyebrows. Ginny just waved at him to answer it. Only one person would knock on her door at 2 a.m., and that was the only other person with a key to the café.

Madelaine gave Paul a nod as she hurried through the entry and into the bedroom to perch on the edge of Ginny's bed. She felt her forehead, and despite the fact that Ginny hadn't run a fever during the entire event, she allowed her mother to "mother" her for a couple of minutes. It was easier than the alternative.

By the time Madelaine had finished replacing her flat pillows with fluffed ones, and sending Paul to fetch aspirin, a glass of water and an ice bag, she finally showed signs of ceasing the theatrics. Unfortunately, then she started the inquisition.

"Are you sure you're feeling all right?"

"I'm fine. Did Sheriff Blackwell find anything?"

Madelaine pursed her lips, and Ginny could tell that her usually relaxed mother was completely put out by the sheriff. "No. There was no 'forced entry'— as he called it—so he has no idea how anyone got in the house. The kitchen floor had been scrubbed with bleach, and they couldn't find any drops of blood outside."

"Did they follow the ATV tracks?"

Madelaine frowned and looked down at the bed. Paul, apparently sensing that something wasn't right, went around to the other side of the bed and sat next to Ginny and across from Madelaine. Finally, she looked back up at Ginny and said, "There were no tracks to follow."

Ginny's jaw dropped. "He covered the ATV tracks? I mean, I know he had time, but why would he bother with something that can't be traced directly back to him?"

"Because then people won't believe you," Paul said, a hard edge to his voice. "Don't you see? There's no proof except your word that you were attacked. The sheriff is probably well on his way to suggesting that you imagined the entire thing."

Madelaine blew out a breath. "The darn fool already has suggested it, and got an earful from me."

Ginny's jaw dropped. "Then who does he think shot at Paul?"

"Poachers," Madelaine said. She looked over at Paul. "You don't seem to think much of that theory."

"No, ma'am, I don't. I know I haven't known Ginny for very long, but she certainly hasn't struck me as someone with mental issues or a case of the dramatics. I believe it happened just as she says."

"Mom?" Ginny asked, unable to keep her voice from quivering just a bit. "You didn't believe the sheriff, did you? You didn't think—"

Madelaine gathered Ginny in her arms in a crushing hug. "Absolutely not. You're the sanest person I know, and I know everyone in this town. Somebody's just got fixated on you and has been real careful to conceal it."

She released Ginny and gave her a stern look. "You have got to be really careful until this guy is caught. I think you ought to move back in with me."

"No. There's no chance that he'll get caught if the sheriff's not looking for him. You're talking about changing my life permanently because of fear."

Madelaine opened her mouth to argue, but Paul interrupted. "She's right," he said. "My best friend was a cop for a long time. If someone's targeting Ginny, moving in with you will only put you both at risk."

Ginny wondered for a minute who Paul was talking about, then realized he was probably referring to himself, and still didn't want Madelaine to know his true profession.

"You don't think I can protect myself?" Madelaine asked, clearly perturbed.

"I think that whoever came after Ginny prepared well and waited for an opportunity. Now that his cover is blown and his objective is known, he may move on."

Ginny looked over at Paul, and he gave her a barely imperceptible shake of his head. He didn't believe that for a second. He was only saying it to alleviate some of Madelaine's fears.

"And regardless of what the sheriff believes," Paul continued, "he didn't strike me as the type of man who would ignore the situation altogether."

"No," Madelaine said. "He'll poke into it from every side like he's always done with any problem in Johnson's Bayou, but I have my doubts about his ability to handle something this serious. The man hasn't been the same since his wife, Meg, died. Do you think him poking into things, even in a cursory manner, is enough to keep someone from trying again?"

"I think it's enough for now," Paul said, "but I think you should install a security system, complete with cameras, at the café and at your home. I also think that as soon as Ginny's up to it, both of you should take a firearms course and keep protection in your home."

"Ha," Madelaine scoffed. "Shows what you know. I was the parish's skeet shooting champion three years running in my younger days, and I promise you, I haven't lost my edge."

Ginny stared at her mom. "You never told me that."

Madelaine gave her a sheepish grin. "My daddy really wanted a son, and when I was the fifth daughter born, he improvised."

"Good," Paul said. "I have a friend in the security business in New Orleans. I can get you a good price on the equipment, but it will probably take a couple of days before they can get here and install it."

"The café's been doing well for years," Madelaine said. "You get me whatever you think will keep us safe, and send me a bill. I've been meaning to do something for a while now, but always managed to keep my head in the sand about the way things have changed since I was a girl."

Madelaine patted Ginny's arm. "Paul and I are going to get out of here and let you get some rest. I've got a change of clothes here that'll do for café work tomorrow. I'll sleep on the couch for what's left of the night."

Paul rose from the bed, taking his cue to leave. "I'll be back when the café opens, unless you want me to come when you start working."

Madelaine rose from the bed and walked around to give Paul a hug. "You're a nice, responsible young man, but you get some sleep. He won't bother us again tonight."

Ginny looked up at Paul and he nodded, agreeing with Madelaine's assessment. "Thank you," Ginny said to Paul. "For everything. If you hadn't come..."

"Don't even think about it," he said. "I'll see you first thing in the morning." He gave Madelaine a nod and left the apartment.

"Back in a minute," Madelaine said and hurried behind him to lock the café doors.

Ginny leaned back on the pillows and stared up at the ceiling. Things had gone from insane to impossible. She hoped that Paul would come up with a plan overnight, because at the moment, she had no idea at all what to do. The entire situation had her so far out of her element that she didn't even recognize her life any more. Her memory, stalkers, car chases, shooters and now, Paul's kiss.

More than anything, Ginny just wanted to go back to the way things were before.

PAUL SLAMMED HIS HAND on his steering wheel and cursed. If it was the last thing he ever did, he was going to catch the man who'd done this to Ginny and make him pay. He'd come into this town expecting it to yield nothing, as all his investigations concerning his sister had gone before. Instead, he'd found a link to his sister in a woman who had his emotions working in overdrive. He'd only intended to get information out of Ginny, but now he found himself drawn into her situation, her life...her, in general. And that was something he definitely hadn't planned on.

He couldn't believe he'd kissed her, and from the

look on her face, she couldn't believe it, either. It had been a stupid, impulsive thing to do given everything that was happening, but at that moment, nothing short of death could have stopped him. Ginny had captured a part of him that he didn't think had existed any longer. A part of him he'd thought he'd closed off after his last failed relationship—a failure that his refusal to give up looking for his sister had contributed to.

But he couldn't think about all of that right now. He had to concentrate on figuring out what happened at the LeBlanc School. There was no doubt in his mind that someone from Ginny's past was trying to prevent her from remembering more than she already had.

He pulled his cell phone from his pocket and pressed speed dial for his partner, Mike. The night owl answered on the first ring.

"What's wrong?" Mike asked, knowing that Paul would never call at 2 a.m. unless something was seriously off.

Paul filled him in on the events of the night, pausing only long enough for Mike to interject a couple of questions and the occasional appreciated threat to the man who'd attacked Ginny.

"Wow, man," Mike said when Paul had finished relaying the night's events. "This is out of control. I don't know what all you've stepped in the middle of, but it stinks to high heaven."

"Got that right."

"You think someone followed you to New Orleans and saw you questioning people at the hospital?" his partner asked.

"I didn't see anyone following me, and I was keeping a close watch. Besides, he couldn't have been following me and watching Ginny. Someone knew she was at her mother's house tonight, and the only way he could have known that was by following them when they left the restaurant."

"Where are you now?"

"I'm parked in front of the café, and I'm not going anywhere. Madelaine is staying with Ginny tonight, but until this is all over, I'm not letting her out of my sight again. Did you get any more information on the people I asked you to check?"

"Yeah, hold on."

The sound of paper rustling came through the phone.

"Got back an interesting hit on your maintenance guy, Saul Pritchard. Every year in January, he deposits a twenty-five-thousand-dollar cashier's check in his bank account. Goes back sixteen years. I tried to trace the checks, but it's a no-go. Someone is clearly covering their tracks."

"No sign of a trust or pension that could be paying him?"

"No way. All the family I could find is dirt-poor, and far as I can tell, he's never worked for a company in his life. No military service, either."

"Sounds like a payoff, and I don't think for a minute it's a coincidence that he's been receiving the checks for sixteen years."

"You think he knows something?"

"Either he knows something or someone's paid him to watch Ginny all these years."

"Watch her for what?"

"In case she started to remember." Paul blew out a breath. "What about the sheriff? He didn't seem like he wanted to light any fires over the situation tonight. In fact, he appeared skeptical about the entire thing."

"Skeptical makes him a cop. And there's nothing criminal about being lazy. Besides, if I didn't know you, what you're really doing there, and if I didn't trust your judgment about Ginny, I would have a hard time swallowing all this myself. It's kinda out there, man."

"You're right. I guess I'm just angry. So I assume you didn't find anything on the sheriff?"

"Not much. He's lived in Johnson's Bayou his entire life. Got a degree in criminology at the university in New Orleans, became a deputy in the town after graduation and married his high school sweetheart, Meg."

"Meg? That must be who Madelaine was talking about when she said the sheriff hadn't been the same since she died. I didn't even think to ask at the time because of everything else going on, but sounds like Madelaine believes his job performance has gone down since her death."

"Could be. She died of cancer years ago. Some rare form with a name I can't pronounce. Looks like they tried most everything to save her, but nothing stuck. They never had any kids."

"Finances?"

"His bank records don't show anything but your typical government pay. He's got a good bit of money amassed, but the house he lives in belonged to his mother and is paid for. He doesn't have any debt and doesn't appear to spend much aside from normal living expenses."

"So he's your typical small-town guy. What about the mayor?"

"He's your typical small-town politician. Married a

woman with an inheritance so that he had the means to get himself into office. A real-estate trust makes regular deposits into their joint bank account every month, so I assume her family had some property they're getting rental money or mineral rights from."

"He's never tried to move up the political ladder?"

"Not that I could find, but that's not unusual. He probably doesn't have what it takes to compete with the cutthroats."

Paul thought about the size and normal scope of Johnson's Bayou before he'd rode into town bringing a passel of problems. "Yeah, you're probably right. Pie-tasting events are probably more his speed."

"So what are you going to do next?"

"I don't know. I've got a lot of facts that don't add up to anything and a lot of missing parts that probably have the answers I need to string it all together."

"You're not falling for her, are you?"

Paul felt his pulse increase just a bit at the question. "No."

"You sure? Because I've seen a picture, and she's not hard on the eyes."

"All I see is a woman in danger," Paul lied, knowing he had already lost part of his heart to Ginny, despite every attempt not to.

"Which just makes you want to protect her more." His partner sighed. "Be careful, man. Don't do anything that you're going to regret when this is all over and you come back to New Orleans to your normal life."

"I don't think anything after this will be normal." He set the phone on the dashboard and slumped down in his seat. He wasn't leaving this parking spot. If people wanted to make something of it, then they could feel free. He had no doubt in Madelaine's ability to set them all straight.

His mind raced through the night's events. The killer was getting bolder but was still very careful. The way he'd covered his tracks took forethought and calm. What troubled Paul the most was the why, not the who. Why try to knock Ginny out instead of just shooting her? Why risk entering the house at all when he could have fired a single shot through the window and killed her then?

Paul had a feeling when he found an answer to the why, the who would be revealed.

HE PEERED AROUND THE alley at the end of the street, watching the man who sat in the truck in front of the café. The vacationer had messed up everything by rescuing Ginny. Even though his plan hadn't gone as he'd expected, it could have been salvaged if the vacationer hadn't shown up. He'd covered his tracks, but that was a small solace to the overall failure the night had been.

They were getting too close. If the man found the other girl, she may remember, too, as he was sure Ginny was starting to do. He hadn't taken the risks sixteen years ago or paid hush money to be exposed when he was on the verge of cashing in everything. It was a real shame the vacationer had come to Johnson's Bayou and given credence to Ginny's fears. If he'd just stayed away, both women may have gotten to live.

Now, he had no option.

Chapter Twelve

Patrons started lining up in front of the café ten minutes before it was due to open. Paul figured most of them had probably checked out of the hotel and were ready to enjoy one last meal of fine Southern cooking, then head back to their homes and jobs in the city. Everyone looked tired but happy, and he could see packages filling the backseats of the cars parked around him. Everyone else who'd visited Johnson's Bayou this week had enjoyed their stay.

Paul had been the harbinger of trouble.

Ginny opened the café a little early, but Paul waited until the sidewalk cleared before making his way inside. He took a seat at the end of the counter, away from the other patrons, but knew that before long, the entire place would fill up. There wasn't going to be much chance to talk to Ginny during work hours, but he at least wanted to see how she was doing after last night.

She rushed to deliver coffee and take the initial orders, but managed to give him a brief smile. Finally, the early birds were settled and she made her way over to where he sat. "How are you feeling?" he asked.

"Fine, physically. Just a little bit of a headache, and I have a knot."

"And other than physically?"

"Worried. Confused. Scared. And I really hate to admit the last one."

"Don't be. I'm not exactly comfortable myself, and this is my job."

Ginny gave him a sympathetic look. "But this is personal."

He felt a tingle in his stomach at her words, then realized she was referring to his search for his sister and not her. "Yeah, that makes it harder. That and knowing I made things worse for you."

"Don't blame yourself. Whatever happened back then, the lid was bound to come off sooner or later, and I was already headed down that path."

"I know, but reality doesn't make me feel any better about this." He took a sip of coffee and tried to clear his mind and organize his thoughts for the day. "What time does the café close?"

"We're closing early today. We usually take a couple days off after the festival. After we close today, we're going to take down the valances. Mom's having new ones made. Painting starts tomorrow. What are you doing today?"

"Not letting you out of my sight, for one. I want to catch this guy, and if he's watching you then I may catch him."

"You're going to sit here all day?"

"I promise to tip well."

Ginny smiled. "And after we close? Are you going to work on valances with me and mom?"

"Maybe, as soon as someone explains exactly what they are."

A bell sounded from the counter between the kitchen and the café, and Madelaine slid plates of steaming food up for delivery. "You work on figuring that out. I'll be back." Ginny hustled over to the counter and started delivering the food as more customers started trickling into the café.

Paul reached for an order pad and pen that sat on the end of the counter. He needed to make some notes on everything. Sometimes writing it all down helped bring it together. But before he started, his cell phone vibrated. His partner.

"It must be important if you're up this early," Paul said when he answered.

"What makes you think I've been to bed yet?"

"Touché. I'll rephrase. It must be important if you're calling me this early instead of going to bed."

"It is. Are you somewhere that you can listen? And you might want to be sitting down for this one."

Paul straightened up on the stool at his partner's serious tone. "I'm good. What's up?"

"I got a call from the lab early this morning. They found fingerprints on that book from the LeBlanc School that matched your sister's logged in the foster care system."

Paul felt a wave of dizziness pass over him. He'd hoped…even almost expected this outcome, but it was still overwhelming. He was close—closer than he'd ever been before to figuring out what happened to his sister, and for some reason, he felt certain the girl from the hospital held the answers he sought. He had to find her, although he had no other leads to that end.

"Paul?" Mike's voice sounded over the phone, reminding him that he was on a call.

"Sorry. I spaced out there for a minute. The lab is certain?"

"Absolutely. This is a huge break."

"I know, but I'm at a dead end on finding the other girl."

His partner blew out a breath. "Maybe not. I've got a college buddy who's an attorney. Let me give him a call later this morning and see what it would take to get information out of the hospital."

"I don't think the fingerprints are enough to convince a judge to violate someone's civil rights."

"Let me try. I'll call as soon as I know, either way."

"Thanks." Paul placed the phone on the counter and stared into his coffee.

"Are you all right?" Ginny's voice sounded in front of him.

"What? Oh, yeah." He leaned forward and said in a lowered voice, "My partner just called. The fingerprints on the book match my sister's."

Ginny covered her mouth with her hand and stared at him for a couple of seconds, her eyes wide. "I can't believe—I mean, I knew it was possible, maybe even probable, but there's still that voice in the back of your head that tells you that it could be something completely different." Ginny lowered her hand and shook her head. "I'm sorry. That didn't make any sense at all."

"It made perfect sense to me. I'm feeling the same way."

"So what do you do now?"

Paul shook his head. "I have no idea. My partner's

going to talk to a lawyer about getting access to the medical records for the girl who went to the hospital that night, but I don't think we have enough to compel a judge to issue a court order."

"You think this other girl has the answers?"

"I hope so. Otherwise, I'm right at the edge, but with nothing left to create the tipping point."

Ginny didn't say a word, but she didn't have to. She knew all too well the position he was in—on the verge of discovery, but without any indication which direction to turn. She refilled his coffee and gave him an encouraging smile before rushing off to take care of the other patrons.

Paul picked up the pen and began to jot down the events from the past couple of days. Something would come to him, he tried to tell himself. It always did, and it would this time.

GINNY LOCKED THE CAFÉ DOOR behind the last of the breakfast crowd, looked at the messy café and sighed. Madelaine came through the kitchen door and plopped onto a stool at the counter, looking as exhausted as she felt.

"I know we should start cleaning up," Madelaine said, "but I just have to sit for a minute and catch my breath. I don't think we've been that busy in years."

Ginny plopped onto a stool next to her. "We were this busy yesterday and the day before. We just weren't this tired."

Paul jumped up from his stool at the end of the counter and made his way over to where they sat. "Why don't you two take a break? I'll start cleanup."

Before Ginny found the strength to protest, he'd already stepped behind the counter and grabbed one of the plastic tubs used to collect dirty dishes. Madelaine looked over at Ginny and raised one eyebrow as Paul went to the first table and started stacking dishes in the tub.

"He may be a keeper," Madelaine said.

Ginny frowned. "Paul, you don't have to help. The dishes aren't going anywhere."

He looked over at them and smiled. "And neither are you two. I've sat at that counter drinking coffee for over four hours now, watching the two of you run ragged. Take a breather."

"No one likes a martyr," Madelaine said and elbowed Ginny in the side. "Besides, he probably drank ten dollars' worth of coffee sitting there."

Paul grinned and hauled the first tub through the kitchen doors. Madelaine looked over at Ginny and smiled. "He's a nice young man," she said. "It's clear that he's worried about you and that he cares about people in general. Being a man, he's probably feeling like he should be doing something about last night."

"That's the sheriff's job," Ginny said.

Madelaine nodded. "Yep, but Paul's still a man. And men don't like feeling they didn't protect their lady."

"I'm not his lady. I just met him."

Madelaine patted her leg. "I know, but I can see he feels bad. If picking up a few dirty dishes makes him feel better, then what's the harm?"

Ginny didn't bother to argue, as she knew all too well that Madelaine was right—Paul did feel guilty. Madelaine just wasn't aware of the real reason why. And besides, it sort of amused her that her electively single mother was giving her advice on what men needed.

They sat in silence for a minute, and Ginny stared out the café window, letting the tension in her neck and back unwind. Then Paul came through the kitchen door carrying two glasses of tea that he placed on the counter in front of them before beginning to bus another table.

"You reading minds back there?" Madelaine asked. "I was just thinking it is hot as heck in here."

Ginny looked over at her mother. It wasn't cold in the café, but Ginny would hardly call it hot. She felt her pulse quicken when she saw the red tint on Madelaine's face. "Mom, are you feeling all right?"

"I'm fine," Madelaine said, but her hand shook as she lifted her glass of tea. "I'm sure it's just my blood pressure. It will be fine once I rest a spell."

"You forgot to bring your medicine with you last night, didn't you?"

"Yes, but stop fussing. You're the one that ought to be fussed over."

Paul brushed against Ginny's arm before she realized he sidled up next to her. "You need to be careful with blood pressure," Paul said. "Why don't I drive out to your house and get your medicine?"

"I don't want to be a bother," Madelaine replied.

"It's no bother, and I know Ginny would feel better about you messing with curtains this afternoon if you'd had your medicine." He glanced over at Ginny and she shot him a grateful look before nodding.

"Please let Paul get your medicine. It won't take him long, and you can rest in the meantime. I can get the rest of the tables. There's only a couple."

"And I already loaded everything in the dish-washer," Paul said.

"Fine," Madelaine said. "It takes more energy than I care to spend to tell you two no." She retrieved her keys from her apron pocket and removed her house key. "My medicine bottle's right next to the kitchen sink. It's the only one there."

Paul slipped the key in his pocket. "Lock the door behind me, and don't let anyone in until I return."

He exited the café but waited next to the front door before Ginny turned the dead bolt behind him. Since she was already standing, Ginny slid the last couple of dishes into the tub and carted them to the kitchen. She was surprised to see that Paul had loaded not only the dishes from the front of the café but also the kitchen dishes into the dishwasher.

She smiled at the clean surfaces and tried to ignore that little trickle of warmth that moved through her every time she allowed her thoughts to dwell on him. But it was hard not to dwell. He was a man of values, principles and responsibility. And Lord help her, he was physically impossible to ignore. Ginny had been with men in the past, but not many, and never had she felt the tingling sensation on her skin the way she did when Paul was near.

Even her mother found him impossible to say no to. If anyone else had insisted she sit on a stool while they cleaned her kitchen, Madelaine would have thrown them out on their ear. Apparently Paul's charm worked on her mother as well as it worked on her.

She sighed and opened the dishwasher to load the remaining dishes. None of that meant a thing because when this was all over, Paul would go back to his job in the city and Ginny would remain in Johnson's Bayou, perhaps a little more enlightened about her past, but still alone.

FIVE MINUTES LATER, Ginny removed the valance from a curtain rod and coughed as dust flew up in her face. "How long has it been since we shook these out?" She handed the dusty material to her mother, who was still resting at the counter, then removed another set.

"Months," Madelaine replied, "but looks like they took on some dust when Saul replaced the counter."

"Oh, yeah, I forgot about that."

"Hmmmpf. Don't know how. Darn man in here every day for a week banging on that wood and stone, driving customers crazy with the noise and me even crazier with his complete dedication to doing everything as slowly as possible."

Ginny smiled. Even at sixty, her mother still operated on only two modes—off and on. She made normal people appear lazy. "He's slow and ornery, but he does nice work."

"That's a fact," Madelaine agreed. "And a darned good thing, or no one would hire him."

Ginny laid the valance on the stone counter and admired the cut pieces, all neatly fit into a beautiful array of size and color, and suddenly, a thought hit her. "Mom, when Saul was working, did he have a key to the café?"

"Of course. I wasn't going to sit here until all hours with the man every night. Noise was so bad you moved back in with me for a stretch, in case you don't remember. Not that it mattered—isn't anything to steal here that's expensive unless you want some commercial cooking equipment. Besides, only thing that came up missing while he was working was lemon chess pie, even though he still swears he didn't eat it."

Ginny nodded, but her mind was elsewhere. "I'm going to grab a soda. Do you want anything?"

"A little more iced tea would be nice."

Ginny walked through the swinging doors into the kitchen and went straight for her mother's desk in the corner. She glanced back at the swinging doors before pulling open the desk drawer. In a plastic container in the back corner of the drawer, she found what she was looking for and dumped the keys into the palm of her hand. It took only a glance for her to know that one of them was the key to her apartment and another a key to Madelaine's house.

Normally, the keys would have been safe there, and it would have been a logical place to keep the spares, as usually only Ginny or Madelaine had a key to the café or were in the kitchen. But Saul had been in there alone for a week, and Ginny hadn't even thought about the spare keys being in the drawer. She'd bet anything Madelaine hadn't, either. He'd had an entire week to make a copy of the keys, and neither Ginny nor Madelaine would have been the wiser. And the hardware store wouldn't even blink at the contractor having keys made.

Ginny prepared the drinks and carried them back into the café, careful to mask the worried look she knew she'd developed after finding the keys. Madelaine dropped the valance she'd been folding onto the counter as Ginny stepped through the doors.

"Thanks," she said gratefully and took a huge swig of the ice-cold tea. "It's humid in here."

Ginny took a sip of her soda and glanced around the café at the remaining valances. "What are you going to do with these?"

"Probably give them to the church. The color's still good on the fabric since I had them dry-cleaned all these years, and they need some new valances for the nursery. They'll look nice, since the walls are pale blue."

"I assume you're going to have them cleaned first?"

"Of course. What kind of Christian gives dirty stuff to a church?" Madelaine laughed. "For that matter, I guess we better check all the seams before I take them to the cleaners and fix anything that's loose."

"Okay." Ginny stretched one of the valances across the counter with the length trailing over the front edge. Slowly, she pulled the fabric toward her, inspecting the hem on the top and bottom of the valance as she pulled. When she got to the end of the valance, she saw a frayed thread below an unusual lump in the fabric.

She felt the fabric and realized that something fairly stiff was inside the one-inch hem. She pulled a bit on the thread and exposed a couple of inches of the seam. "There's something inside the hem on this one," Ginny said.

Madelaine looked over and nodded. "Sometimes people sew a cardboard piece or something else stiff in the hem to make them hang right. Although...there doesn't appear to be any in this one."

"The seam's already loose. Do you want me to take it out?"

"Might as well. It's probably deteriorated anyway after all this time."

Ginny stuck her fingers into the seam and tried to

pull the folded paper, but all she accomplished was
tearing off a piece. She tossed the scrap on the counter
and prepared to tackle the hem again when something
caught her eye.

The scrap had writing on it.

She picked up the piece and studied it closely, but all
she could make out was the letter "s." Her pulse quickened and she pulled the thread to widen the opening
in the hem. It could be nothing. It could be a grocery
list.

But everything in her body screamed that this scrap
of paper that had been tucked in a valance hem for sixteen years was very important. She wriggled her fingers into the hem and grasped the paper, then slowly
eased it out from the fabric. Her hands shook as she
unfolded the yellowed paper.

Please help u

Ginny gasped and slid the scrap with the *s* across
the counter and fit it into the gap at the end of the sentence.

"What's wrong?" Madelaine's voice sounded right
next to her and Ginny jumped. She reached for the
papers, hoping to slide them off the counter before
Madelaine could see, but it was too late.

"Oh, my." Madelaine stared in horror at the child-
like print. "Those poor girls."

"It could be anything," Ginny tried to rationalize.
"It could be from homework or stories made up for
fun."

Madelaine narrowed her eyes at Ginny. "It could
be, but that's not what you believe. I can see it in your
face, Ginny. You know something. You and Paul are up
to something. I've kept quiet about it because it didn't

appear to be anything serious and I thought you deserved a bit of fun, but I want to know what's going on. I'm making it my business now."

Ginny stared at Madelaine for a moment, not even knowing where to start, and when she finally opened her mouth to speak, a knock sounded on the café door. They both looked over to see Paul standing in front of the café and giving them a wave.

"Excellent timing," Madelaine said as she walked to the front door to let him in.

Paul stepped through the door into the café and gave Madelaine a big smile. Madelaine scowled and said, "I want you two to tell me everything you've been up to. And you're going to start."

She pointed her finger at Paul, who now stared at her with a deer-in-the-headlights expression. "Who are you, really? What do you want with my daughter? And what happened to those girls at that school?"

Chapter Thirteen

Paul stared at Madelaine, at a complete loss for words. He looked over at Ginny, who stood frozen at the counter and wondered what in the world had happened to set her mother off. "Did I miss something?" he asked.

Ginny nodded. "Yeah. You need to look at this." She explained the stack of valances on the counter and pointed to the note she'd found inside the hem.

Paul felt his blood go cold as he read the words. "I'm sorry that I wasn't up-front with you," he said to Madelaine, "but Ginny and I didn't want to worry you, especially because we don't really know anything concrete yet."

"About what happened to those girls?" Madelaine asked.

"Yes," Paul replied. "That's part of it, but there's a lot more. Maybe we should all sit. This is going to take a while."

Madelaine slid into a chair at one of the tables and Paul and Ginny took a seat across from her.

Paul handed her her blood pressure medicine. "Maybe you should take that first."

Madelaine narrowed her eyes at him and downed a pill with her tea. He could tell she was still put out, but maybe by the time he'd finished explaining everything to her, she'd understand why Ginny had been less than honest.

He started at the beginning with his real reason for coming to Johnson's Bayou. Madelaine listened in rapt and sometimes shocked attention as he covered finding Ginny, their visit to the house, Ginny's recent feelings of being watched and her suspicions that someone had been in her apartment. Then he told her about the shooter from the night they visited the old school and his suspicions about Ginny's attacker the night before.

The color vanished from Madelaine's face as he talked. "I can't believe someone tried to kill you—twice," Madelaine said, her voice almost hoarse. "And you didn't tell me."

"Oh, Momma," Ginny said, "the last thing I wanted was to put you in danger. You know if the situation was reversed you would have done the same thing."

Madelaine wasn't quite convinced, but she didn't argue. "Are you starting to remember?" she asked Ginny.

Ginny nodded. "I think so, but it's more of a feeling than a memory. Sometimes, I feel like someone's watching or someone's in danger, but the fear is almost like that of a child afraid of monsters, not an adult afraid of a predator. I know that sounds odd. Every once and a while, I look at something and just for a millisecond, I have this flash like I'm going to remember and then it's gone."

Madelaine looked at Paul. "Do you think she's going to remember?"

"I think she'll eventually remember something or feel a familiarity when seeing certain people or things that weren't there before. It's hard to say if any of that will ever become clear."

Madeleine reached across the table and took Ginny's hand in hers. "I wish you would have talked to me about all this, but I understand why you didn't. You're a good girl, Ginny, and the best daughter anyone could ask for. I know you need to do this, but I need you to come out of it alive. For me. I'm just gonna be selfish and say it. So if it comes down to those girls resting in peace or you being alive, you know where my vote lies."

Ginny brushed at the tears on her cheek with her free hand. "We were being careful. As careful as we could be, but it didn't stop him from coming after me. This was bound to happen when I started remembering. He started after me right after I started to remember."

Madeleine stared at her. "You're saying he's been stalking you for what—months, years? And we've never noticed? How can that be?"

Ginny glanced at Paul and said, "I don't think he had to stalk me."

Madeleine looked confused for a moment, as if she was waiting for Ginny to finish her thought, then it dawned on her exactly what Ginny was saying. Her hands flew up to cover her mouth. "It's someone we know. That's what you're telling me. That someone you've probably served coffee every week of your life is trying to kill you."

"He must have been watching closely and noticed a change when I started having those flashes," Ginny said. "My going to look at the school just reinforced what he was already thinking. I'm lucky Paul was here when it started, otherwise, I don't know how things would have turned out. I had no idea the magnitude of what I was stepping into."

"Neither did I," Paul said to Madelaine. "I swear to you, I had no idea of all the trouble my investigation or Ginny's remembering would cause. Someone has been hiding a dark secret for a long time, and even though we have no idea what the secret is or who's hiding it, we've made ourselves targets."

"So that's it?" Madelaine said, a bit of an edge to her voice. "You just intend to walk around with targets on your back?"

"Absolutely not," Paul said. "I intend to find out what happened sixteen years ago. Ginny will never be safe until it's all exposed."

"I want to know what you're doing every second of this." Madelaine gave Paul a look that clearly said no arguing was allowed. "I'm an old woman and not fit for running from shooters, but I expect to know everything you two are doing. I need to know when to send backup. You can't continue this without a backup plan."

"I agree," Paul said. "The stakes have increased dramatically, and it will make me feel better knowing someone I trust knows what we're doing and when to call for help. I can't tell you what that means yet, though. First, we have to determine our next step."

"First," Ginny said, "in addition to the security system Paul's getting for us, I want to change the locks on my apartment. Every time the café is empty, someone has the opportunity to get in there. I know locks won't keep people out if they really want in, but it will

make it a lot harder to get in without exposing himself."

Madelaine narrowed her eyes at Ginny. "You think Saul took my key when he was building those countertops? That's why you asked about him earlier. Is the key to your apartment still in my desk drawer?"

"Yes, along with a key to your house, but he had plenty of time to copy them and put them back."

Madelaine's shoulders slumped. "I'm sorry. I didn't even think—"

"Of course not," Ginny interrupted. "Why would you?"

"So you think it's Saul? Is he the one?" Madelaine asked.

"We don't know," Paul said. "It could have been him, or someone could have dropped by to talk to him and he let them in. There's really no way to know for certain without asking, and I don't want to alert him. I'm going to be watching him closely, though, especially as he'll be here painting."

Madelaine shook her head. "This is so much more complicated than I imagined. You're right. Anyone in town could have stopped by and he'd have let them right in. There could be any number of keys out there by now."

"Don't worry about it," Paul said. "I'll visit the hardware store and pick up a new lock. The hardware comes with two keys, so that way no one else will get a chance to touch them but me and the two of you. And while I'm at the hardware store, I'll make sure everyone there knows I'm changing out the locks here so that bit of information can work its way around town. With any luck, it will filter to your attacker so he'll know that avenue is closed or at least infinitely more difficult to disguise."

"Why would people gossip about my changing the lock on my apartment?" Ginny asked. "This is a small town, but really, more is going on than that."

Madelaine laughed. "They won't care about you changing your lock, but they'll certainly talk about a handsome, young stranger doing it for you, especially after he rescued you last night." She gave Paul an approving nod. "You're a sharp young man."

Paul sighed. "I wish that were true. If I were sharper, perhaps I'd find my sister."

Madelaine's expression grew sad. "You're sure Ginny's not your sister, right?"

"She has the wrong eye color."

"But you think your sister was at the school?"

"Yes. I think that's where Ginny got the design she uses for her jewelry. My sister drew it on everything."

Madelaine's eyes widened. "Oh! What about the other girl? The one who the firefighters pulled out alive?"

"So far, I haven't been able to locate her. My partner tracked her to the hospital in New Orleans, but I talked to some of the people who cared for her back then. That's where I was yesterday—why I wasn't here protecting Ginny. But it was a dead end. No one knows where the girl went after she was released from the hospital."

"I do." Madelaine rose from the booth, an excited look on her face. "Or at least, I know someone who probably will. Give me a minute."

Madelaine ran into the kitchen, and a couple of seconds later they heard her talking on the phone. Her voice was high-pitched and had an excited tone, but they couldn't make out exactly what she was saying. Paul tried not to get his hopes up, but it was impossible. If Madelaine had another lead for him to follow, it might be the break he'd been looking for.

Several agonizing minutes later, she ran back into the café, her face flushed with excitement. She handed Paul a piece of paper with a name on it. "That's her," Madelaine said. "I had a friend who worked at the rehab center where she went after the hospital discharged her. She called me as soon as the girl arrived to ask about the school and the fire. She was trying to put together what had created her condition, hoping that would give her some insight into designing therapy for her."

"And she's still there?"

"No. She was in a coma for quite a long time in the hospital, but after her burns healed, she just woke up one day. After that, they sent her to rehab, which is when my friend got her. They had to retrain her on how to read and write, and my friend said she couldn't remember a thing about her life before the fire. Once she was ready for a normal life, they petitioned the court for a name and she went to live with a foster family."

Madelaine pointed to the paper. "That's the name she chose. Of course, that was years ago and there's a good chance she's married now, but I figure you could find that out, right?"

Paul stared at the name on the paper. *Kathy Stevens.* His heart leapt when he read the name. Kathy. Could she have forgotten everything but her first name?

"I'll call this in to my partner and have him start

searching immediately." He looked over at Madelaine. "I don't know how to thank you."

Madelaine's eyes teared up and she waved a hand in dismissal. "Don't thank me yet. Thank me if we find out it's your sister."

Paul pulled out his phone and called Mike. He'd probably wake him up at this hour of the morning, but it was worth it. Once his sleepy partner answered, he rattled off the name then disconnected the call, trying to keep his excitement to a minimum by folding valances.

He didn't have to wait long. Ten minutes later, Mike called back. He'd found Kathy Stevens.

PAUL LOOKED ANXIOUSLY at Ginny, took a deep breath and slowly blew it out. Ginny reached for his hand and gave it a squeeze. "I know I said I wasn't going to get my hopes up, but I lied."

"It would be impossible not to be hopeful," Ginny said. "It's a long shot, but the chance is still there. You'll never know, though, if you don't ring the doorbell."

Paul nodded. "You're right." He reached his free hand up and rang the doorbell.

They heard footsteps inside and a couple of seconds later, a pretty woman with her long brown hair pulled into a ponytail opened the door. She smiled at them and asked, "Can I help you?"

Paul felt his knees weaken. It was her. Older, more mature, but there was no mistaking his sister's face. *Concentrate. Don't scare her.* "Are you Kathy Stevens?"

"Yes, but it's Kathy Landry now." The woman

looked back and forth expectantly from Paul to Ginny. "Is something wrong?"

She doesn't remember me. Paul struggled to control the wave of disappointment that coursed through him. Ginny squeezed his hand and he tried to focus. "My name is Paul Stanton. Does that mean anything to you?"

Kathy frowned. "No…no, I don't think so. Should it?"

This is wrong. Just say you made a mistake and leave her to her life. Clearly she's moved on and isn't hurting about the past. Dredging it up will only cause her pain. "My mistake," Paul said, his voice shaky. "I thought you were someone else." He glanced over at Ginny, whose face fell at his declaration. "Let's go."

He started to turn when Kathy grabbed the sleeve of his shirt. "Wait!" She stared at him for several seconds, her eyes narrowed on his face. Her expression was puzzled, as if she were trying to put the pieces together. Then she gasped and a flush rushed up her neck and over her face. She put both hands up to cover her mouth. "Oh, my God. I remember. Paul…you're Paul."

Kathy looked back into the house and yelled, "John! Come here quick!"

A fit, handsome man hurried up beside her, a worried look on his face. "What's wrong? Are these people bothering you?"

"No," Kathy began to cry and pointed to Paul. "This is my brother. I remember him. I have a brother." She stepped forward and placed her arms around Paul's neck. Paul glanced at her bewildered husband, then hugged her back as she began to sob, unable to hold back his own tears.

It took several minutes to stop the hugging and crying long enough to explain the basics to Kathy's husband, but Ginny took the lead and filled in the gaps. John's expression went from confused to shocked to overwhelmed in a matter of seconds, and he ushered all of them inside to the living room to sit. He took a seat on the couch next to his wife and put his arm around her.

"I can't believe it," he said and gave his wife a squeeze. "Kathy never remembered anything about the past except her first name. We didn't even know she had a brother, and now, for you to be here…I'm sorry, I'm rambling. I don't even know what to say."

"It's a miracle," Kathy said and brushed the tears from her cheeks with the back of her hand. "I'd given up trying to remember a long time ago. I figured if no one was looking for me, then there wasn't much of importance to recall, so I just moved on. As if my life began on the day I left the hospital."

Ginny sniffed and Paul instantly realized that what Kathy had just described was Ginny's life, too. They'd had parallel experiences starting with the same tragedy. He took Ginny's hand in his own and looked over at her, hoping to convey his understanding with a look. She gave him a small smile.

"I still can't believe it," Kathy said. "All these years. What happened? How did you find me? Oh, my…I have so many questions. I don't know where to start."

Paul recounted their childhood to Kathy, who cried again over their parents' deaths and was suitably horrified by the actions of child protective services. She asked a lot of questions that Paul could answer about their life with their parents and even more that he couldn't answer about what happened afterward.

"You have no memory of the time before you left the hospital?" Paul asked.

"Not really. I mean, I know I was at the school and rescued from the fire. Sometimes I get flashes of memory—like seconds in time—but vivid, like a movie. I think it's during the time I was at the school. It was an old, huge house with cypress trees surrounding it. I remember sewing and playing in a huge yard with other girls. But nothing concrete. Just snippets."

Kathy shook her head. "When I first saw you, nothing registered, but then when you were about to leave, something hit me and suddenly I knew. I can't remember a single thing about our childhood, but I knew with certainty that you were my brother."

Kathy looked over at Ginny. "I'm sorry, we've just been going on and on. Are you Paul's wife?"

"No," Ginny said. "I just met Paul this week when he came to Johnson's Bayou looking for you. I…I'm like you. I don't know my past. I appeared in Johnson's Bayou the day after the fire at the school, but like you, no one ever came looking for me."

"Oh, honey," Kathy said, "I am so sorry. Is there anything we can do? Surely, if Paul found me, he can get answers for you."

"I'm going to get answers for Ginny," Paul assured her. "I knew I was going to help her once I heard her story, but now, it's become even more critical."

Kathy and John frowned. "What's wrong?" Kathy asked. "Are you sick?"

"No," Paul answered, "but I think she's in danger. She's started to remember—flashes of memory like you describe—but nothing concrete. Unfortunately, someone has been paying close attention to Ginny and noticed that she changed when the flashes began. I think the fire at the LeBlanc School was intentional—that those girls were all murdered. Whoever has kept it hidden all these years is threatened by Ginny's returning memories. There have already been two attempts on her life."

John jumped up from the couch, his face flushed with red. "And you came here? You knowingly exposed us to danger? What's wrong with you?"

Paul shook his head, not blaming the other man in the least for his anger. "You were already in danger. I'm sure whoever is watching Ginny has always known where Kathy was. He's probably kept a close eye on her all these years."

"But before now, he had no reason to assume she knew anything."

"And he still doesn't," Paul said. "He doesn't know you're my sister, and even if he finds out we came here today, he has no reason to believe you could recall anything at all. When I leave here today, I won't contact you or return until this whole thing is settled. Okay?"

John ran one hand through his hair, still clearly unnerved at the entire situation. "Yeah. Yeah, I guess you're right. I'm just a little out of my element here."

"We're all a little out of our element," Paul reassured him. "My work usually isn't personal, so it's different for me, too."

"What if I remember something?" Kathy asked. "I haven't in all these years, but what if now things start to come back—things that might help you figure out what happened? How do I get in touch with you?"

Paul pulled a card from his wallet and handed it to Kathy. "That has all my contact information, but just to be safe, don't use your home phone, cell phone or computer to contact me. Use a workplace phone or a public internet connection."

"Is that really necessary?" John asked.

"Probably not," Paul replied, "but I don't want to take any chances. If whoever is watching Ginny thinks this is a dead end, he'll leave you alone."

At least, that's what Paul hoped.

THE MAN WATCHED AS Paul and Ginny pulled away from the woman's house. How had they found her? The nurse promised him she hadn't said a word. Had she lied? Or had they found someone else who knew how to find the woman? Did the woman remember anything when she saw them?

He'd watched the woman over the years, as he'd watched Ginny. Neither had shown signs of remembering, so he'd left them alone to their new lives. He'd been altruistic, thinking himself a great man of mercy. But now, that decision was coming back to haunt him.

If he'd killed the girls back then, it would have drawn attention from the police, but without any evidence, ultimately, the police would have blamed the missing headmistress for the crimes. Sixteen years was a long time for someone to wait to start killing again, and the police would definitely be able to make the connection between Ginny and the woman, especially now that they were both aware of each other's existence.

He knew the man, Paul Stanton, was lying about his real profession as a detective, but why had he lied? Had

Ginny paid him to unravel the secrets of her memories? Or was the other woman really his sister, as he'd told the nurse?

And what of Ginny's mother? He'd been keeping a close watch on Madelaine, but the older woman showed no signs of being aware that her daughter was involved in anything outside of her normal routine and spending a little time with a vacationing stranger. Certainly, she hadn't appeared worried, as he was certain she would have been if she'd known Ginny's memory was returning. That was a good thing, he decided.

The fewer people that were aware of what was going on, the lower the body count when it was all over.

Chapter Fourteen

Paul sank down on the couch in Ginny's apartment, still unable to believe everything that had happened that day. Ginny seemed only slightly less dazed than he felt, and he heard her now, clinking glasses around in the kitchen. A couple of seconds later, she handed him a beer and slumped down on the couch next to him with a glass of wine.

"I'm out of Scotch," she said. "Tough week around here for Scotch."

Paul laughed. "It's so surreal, you know?"

"I feel like I've lived a year in the past twenty-four hours."

Paul stared at her, surprised that she'd so easily verbalized what he was feeling, and then comforted by the knowledge that someone else really got it. In all the time he'd imagined this moment, he'd never imagined sharing it with someone else. But now that he'd met Ginny, he couldn't imagine it any other way. "That's it exactly. When I think about everything that's happened since I arrived here, it seems almost impossible that it's all been in the span of a few days."

"Well, I guess in all fairness, it's been building for sixteen years."

"True."

Ginny took a sip of wine, then looked over at him and smiled. "You found your sister." She held up her wine glass and he clinked his beer against it, unable to control the grin that spread across his face.

"I found my sister," he said. A rush of emotion overwhelmed him—happiness at finally finding her, sadness at their lost childhood and everything she'd been through, and most of all, fear that the past wasn't yet behind them.

"How does it feel? I mean…you don't have to answer if you don't want to—"

"It feels incredible! It's like everything you can possibly feel is all happening at the same time."

Ginny nodded. "Overwhelming emotion. I can imagine, especially after all this time and given all the circumstances surrounding it." She placed her hand on his. "I know today wasn't exactly the reunion you were hoping for, but as soon as we figure all this out, you'll be able to have the relationship with your sister that you want."

Paul placed his beer on the coffee table. "You always know the perfect thing to say—like you've known me forever." He stroked her cheek with his hand. "You're a special woman, Ginny. Like no one I've ever known before."

Her face tingled at his touch and a quivering began deep inside her. She knew he was going to kiss her and that she should prevent it, but no amount of logic was going to override her body's desire for him. She longed to have his hands, his lips on her, making her whole.

When his lips touched hers, the quivering that had

begun at her center radiated out to every square inch of her body. Warmth followed, and as he deepened the kiss, their tongues dancing together, she thought her clothes would catch on fire from the heat of her skin. She wanted this man. Since meeting him, her entire life had changed—become fuller, more immediate. It was as if she hadn't really started to live until this week…until Paul Stanton.

"I want you, Ginny," he whispered.

"Yes," she said and wrapped her arms around him.

He surprised her by lifting her completely off the couch and carrying her into the bedroom. She thought he'd place her on the bed, but instead he lowered her beside it and kissed her again as they stood, their bodies pressed together. He ran his hands down her sides to catch the hem of her shirt, then pulled it over her head in one fluid motion.

She surprised herself by returning the favor as he unsnapped her bra and let it drop to the floor. He pulled her in close to him and kissed her again, and the feel of his skin on hers sent another rush of heat through her body. With total abandon, Ginny unbuttoned her jeans and stepped out of them. She wanted him, and no amount of common sense was about to interfere with what her body had already set in motion.

Paul removed his jeans, his eyes doing a slow scan of her body from head to toe. She was surprised to find that she didn't feel the least bit self-conscious. The desire was so clear in his expression that it made her feel sexy and powerful. She reached into the nightstand and pulled out protection. There was rarely opportunity to use any, but Ginny believed in being prepared for anything, even a long shot like Paul Stanton.

He rolled on the protection then lay on the bed and pulled her down beside him. His hand ran down her shoulders and across her breasts, and she closed her eyes, savoring every touch.

"You are so beautiful. I want to explore every inch of you," he whispered.

Ginny felt the fire flame inside her at his words and knew she wouldn't last long enough for an exploration. "Not this time," she said. "I want you now. You can explore on round two."

His eyes widened and she felt him stiffen even more against her thigh. He kissed her again, then whispered, "Whatever the lady wants."

He moved on top of her and she opened herself to him, her body aching for him to enter. When he pushed slowly into her, she gasped and clutched his back. He moaned and lowered his head to kiss her again as he started the rhythmic movement that soon sent both of them over the edge.

Her body exploded with sensation as they climaxed and she cried out, digging her nails into the tender skin on his back. He thrust into her one last time, and then was still. He remained motionless above her for a couple of seconds and she wrapped her arms around him, enjoying the heavy weight of him on top of her, then he slid to the side and gathered her in his arms.

He kissed her softly and, despite having just been sent over the edge in the most spectacular fashion ever, her body still tingled as he kissed her, touched her. Ginny smiled and ran her hands down his bare backside, glad it was fairly early in the night.

Clearly, they weren't yet done.

She hid under the bed in the older girl's room when the lady came to gather them. Even though the lady had always been nice, she scared Ginny, but not as much as the man. She'd been at the house only two days, and so far, she'd been treated well, but Ginny knew something wasn't right. With the lady or the man.

The lady's words were kind, but there was an edge to her voice that belied her feelings. The man only smiled. Always smiling. But the smile gave Ginny the chills.

As soon as the lady left, Ginny snuck out the bedroom window and climbed down the trellis. The man was there, too, gathering the girls and taking them downstairs. Ginny didn't know what would happen downstairs, but she didn't want to be there. Not with the man.

She stepped off the trellis behind a bush with pretty pink flowers and peered between the leaves to make sure the backyard was empty. Of all the places she'd seen at the house, Ginny liked the backyard the best so far. It had stone walkways and benches hidden by giant bushes with sweet-smelling flowers.

That afternoon in the backyard, Ginny pretended that she'd been whisked off to a land far away, where fairies sprinkled magic dust on the flowers to make them smell good. Ginny was a princess and everyone in the kingdom adored her. The fairy kingdom didn't have a wicked witch or a bad man. Not like the house.

The night air seemed to still as she stepped out of her hiding place and scurried for the stone path that led to the other side of the yard where the fountain awaited. It was a hot night, and Ginny already anticipated how the cool water of the fountain would feel on her bare feet. She'd just reached the end of the path when something flashed in the corner of her eye.

She turned toward the house and saw flickering light in a tiny decorative window of one of the downstairs rooms. The light jumped and danced on the other side of the sheer curtain and seemed to call to Ginny to step closer. Entranced by the dancing firelight, Ginny crept up to the house and pulled a brick over from the landscaping in front of the window. Standing on her tiptoes on top of the brick, Ginny could just peer over the window ledge and into the room.

The candles that created the dancing light didn't look magical in the room surrounding the girls. Ginny tensed as the bad man stepped into the room then gasped as he grabbed one of the girls from the circle of candlelight and held her down on the table. The bad man wore a black robe and a mask, but Ginny still knew it was him. When he raised his hand over his head, she saw the flash of metal from a knife.

She opened her mouth to scream but no sound came out. A trickle of warm liquid ran down her leg and onto her bare foot. The other girls screamed and began to run, knocking the candles over in their panic. The bad man pushed the girl off the table and ran through the door with the woman. The door closed behind the girls and they pounded on it, but it didn't budge.

The rug went up in flames and the red wallpaper began to peel from the walls, making it look as if the walls were bleeding. The door was locked. There was no other window save the tiny one that Ginny looked through. The girls were trapped.

There was a shout to her left and as she spun

around, she lost her balance and fell off the brick, slamming into the cold, hard dirt. She sprang up from the ground and ran through the garden to the swamp. She heard shouting behind her, but she didn't stop to listen. She just ran, the thorns and branches tearing at her bare skin.

The screams of the girls reverberated in her mind, driving her forward in a frenzy. It was as if she believed that she could outrun their cries.

GINNY WAKENED SCREAMING, her arms flailing against the man who was attacking her. Her heart pounded and her mind yelled that it was all over for her—that the end had come.

"Ginny!" Paul's voice sounded beyond the screams and she focused on it, allowing the screams to fade away. Finally, she saw him in front of her, both hands on her shoulders, shaking them, his fear evident.

"Paul. Oh, my God!" Ginny threw her arms around him, and he hugged her close until her fear subsided enough for her to talk.

"Must have been one heck of a nightmare," Paul said.

Ginny released him and leaned back so that she could see his face. "It was horrible." She recounted what she'd dreamed to Paul, but no matter how vivid or concise the words she chose, they seemed trite in comparison to the horror she'd seen.

"Do you think it was my memory? Or was it all a bad dream?"

Paul shook his head. "I wish I knew. Did you recognize the man from the dream?"

Ginny's mind flashed back to the dream, as if rolling a film in reverse. "No." She frowned. "In my dream, I know he's bad, but I don't see his face. My mind can't focus in on the features. Why is that?"

"Maybe because it was so horrific you blocked out the details. Maybe because it didn't really happen so you couldn't imagine some details with clarity."

"The girls did die in that room. That one with the little window."

"Yes, but you already knew that. That fact could have filtered into your dream, along with a bad man with a butcher knife."

"My attacker last night," Ginny said. "You think my mind could have taken all those details and created a nightmare combining them all. So it wasn't real."

"We don't know that for sure, but I promise you, we're going to find out."

Ginny nodded and lay back down in bed. Paul lay next to her, his arm wrapped protectively around her. Her body relaxed as the heat from his body warmed hers, but her mind whirled with unanswered questions, unanswered horrors.

PAUL SAT ON HIS REGULAR STOOL in the corner of the café, eating a truly fabulous cinnamon roll and watching Ginny as she tallied receipts from the day before. It was early, but this morning the café was empty, awaiting the arrival of Saul Pritchard to get started with the painting. Madelaine had initially wanted to put off her remodeling plans, but Paul pressed her to go ahead with them. It would give him an opportunity to observe Pritchard without drawing attention to the fact.

Ginny's brow scrunched in concentration as she tapped the keys on the adding machine. She'd lain awake for hours last night after her dream, finally drifting off just an hour before the alarm sounded, startling them out of sleep. He'd waited until her breathing was rhythmic and deep before finally allowing himself to slip into slumber with her. The skin around her eyes was darker than the rest, the result of two nights of troubled and lost sleep, but this morning, she'd popped right out of bed when the alarm sounded and gone through her morning routine as if nothing had happened.

Including nothing between them.

Before the nightmare, their night together had been nothing short of incredible for Paul, and he'd thought she felt the same way. But once the morning light crept into her tiny apartment, it was as if a gate slowly closed on the passionate woman from the night before. She was pleasant, as always, but any sign of intimacy was gone. Paul hoped she didn't regret what had happened between them, and at first opportunity, he was going to talk to her about it. The last thing he wanted to do was add to Ginny's worries.

He briefly wondered if she thought he'd spent the night with her only because he was riding on the high of finding his sister, and he hoped that wasn't the case. He was drawn to Ginny in a way he'd never been with any other woman. All his adult life he felt he'd been searching for something besides his sister. With Ginny, he felt as if he'd found that missing piece of himself.

Madelaine hurried into the café from the kitchen with two big cardboard boxes and placed them on a table. "Do you mind helping me?" she asked Paul. "I need to get all the stuff off the tables so Saul can cover them for the painting. I should have done it last night."

"Of course." Paul hopped off his stool and grabbed a box. "Things have been a little crazy around here, but they're going to get better."

Madelaine gave him a quick hug. "You don't know how happy I was when Ginny told me you'd found your sister. And that she remembers you, even a little. It's a miracle."

Paul smiled and started removing napkin holders and salt and pepper shakers from the table and placing them in the box. "I agree. It's all been a little overwhelming. I've looked for so long, and then it's like it hit me all at once."

Madelaine nodded. "I have to believe good things are coming for us all. We just need the dust to settle a bit." There was a knock at the café door and Madelaine glanced at the clock and frowned. Saul wasn't due for another ten minutes, but with the shades drawn, they couldn't see who was standing outside.

Madelaine unlocked the door and opened it to find Mayor Daigle standing outside. She waved him inside, and he gave everyone a big smile before his gaze came to rest on Ginny.

"I just heard about what happened to you night before last," he said. "I am so sorry to hear it and came by first thing to see if there was anything I could do."

"Thank you," Ginny said, "but I'm fine. I was just shaken up a bit."

"Of course you were! I called Sheriff Blackwell as soon as I heard this morning. Got him right out of bed, I did. I cannot believe something like this happened in Johnson's Bayou and he didn't tell me. I have a duty to this community and its people, I told him." The mayor looked righteously indignant.

Madelaine coughed and Paul could tell she was holding in a smile. "No use getting in a dander over it," Ginny said. "Likely Sheriff Blackwell was thinking it was his duty to keep his trap shut about an ongoing investigation."

Mayor Daigle appeared a bit mollified. "Perhaps so. Man's rigid, that's for sure." The mayor stood there silent for several seconds, his gaze shifting among them. Paul could tell the man was just itching for them to provide him some more fodder for gossip, but it was as if they'd all made an unspoken pact to remain silent.

Finally the silence grew unbearable and Mayor Daigle gave them all his big, phony smile again. "Well, I've already taken up too much of you folks' time and I know you got painting going on today. You let me know if there's anything I can do."

"We will," Ginny said. "Thanks for stopping by."

The mayor gave Paul a final glance, then allowed Madelaine to usher him out of the café. She'd hardly closed the door behind him before they all started laughing.

"The look on his face," Madelaine howled, "when none of us would give him any details."

"Priceless," Paul agreed.

Ginny shook her head. "That silence was incredibly uncomfortable, but the man seems to specialize in creating it. Why doesn't he get that he's being intrusive?"

"He gets it," Paul said. "He just doesn't care."

"Yep," Madelaine agreed. "Man's always been nosy. Always in everyone's business."

Another knock sounded at the door, and this time Madelaine glanced at the clock then flew into overdrive, plopping table items into the box. "Darn, he's here and we're not done."

"I'll get it," Paul said as Madelaine hurried to open the door and let Saul in. Ginny joined him in clearing the rest of the tables, and Paul tried to make an unobtrusive assessment of the contractor.

Saul stepped around Madelaine and scanned the café, scowling. "Stuff's gotta be off all the tables and the walls. Don't know why you called me to work when you weren't ready."

"We're almost done," Madelaine assured him. "It will just take a few minutes."

"I'll just step out and have a cigarette while you do. Still charging you for the time, though."

Madelaine looked back at Ginny and Paul and rolled her eyes as Saul made his way out of the café. "The man doesn't know subtlety. Do you really think he could be involved in all this?"

Paul shrugged. "I've seen stranger." He looked out the window and watched as Saul lit a cigarette and leaned against a pole on the covered sidewalk. The contractor moved slowly, almost lazily, his eyes sweeping the street with casual observation. He hadn't even glanced in Paul's direction when he was inside the café and hardly looked troubled now. If he was involved in the happenings in Johnson's Bayou, he was either a fantastic actor or had no blood pressure at all.

After they hauled the boxes to the kitchen, Madelaine waved him inside. As he righted himself from the pole, Paul noticed he favored his right leg for just a second. He grabbed a box of supplies out of the bed of his truck and made his way inside, still not increasing his pace, but no longer favoring the leg. As the man pulled a roll of masking tape from the box, it occurred to Paul that now was the golden opportunity to do a little poking around at Saul's home. The contractor would be at the café all day, and if he left for any reason, Ginny or Madelaine could call and alert Paul.

Paul motioned Ginny back to the kitchen. As soon as the door was safely closed behind them, he whispered, "I saw him favoring his right leg, but only for a bit."

Ginny shook her head. "He's always favored that leg. Some injury from a million years ago. I'd guess he's got arthritis in it now. It disappears once he moves for a while."

Paul felt a flash of disappointment but then caught himself. Just because Saul had an old injury didn't mean he couldn't also have a new one. Paul leaned in close to Ginny and whispered his plan to check out Saul's house. Ginny's eyes widened.

"Are you sure it's safe?" she asked.

"It's as safe now as it's ever going to be."

Ginny pulled her cell phone from her pocket. "I'll turn the volume all the way up to be sure I hear calls. If anything happens, you let me know." Her apprehension was clear.

Paul nodded and they walked back into the front of the café. "Madelaine," Paul called across the café, "I'm going to purchase those new locks for you, now. Is there any particular finish you want?"

Madelaine looked momentarily confused by Paul's announcement, but then she must have remembered their plan to spread the word about the new locks to the residents of Johnson's Bayou. "Nickel is nice and would be a big improvement over that dated gold."

Madelaine glanced at Saul and turned slightly to ensure her back was to him. "Be sure and get two for my house and one for Ginny's apartment as well as the back door to the café." She gave Paul a wink. "Do you need me to write it all down?"

"Nope," Paul said and smiled at Madelaine. "I'm going to run a couple of errands," he told Ginny, "so I'll be back a bit later."

Ginny only nodded but he noticed she stiffened slightly as he bent in to kiss her cheek. Was it nerves over him investigating Saul's house, or was it because of last night?

Too many unanswered questions lurking in his mind, Paul jumped in his truck and tried to focus on one thing at a time. First, he'd pay a visit to Saul's house. The surly contractor was unlikely to take a break soon as he'd just started to work, leaving Paul with the perfect opportunity to poke around his place.

He'd already gotten Saul's home address from Mike and had mapped it on the internet, originally intending to spend some time shadowing the man. This was an even better opportunity, once you ignored the fact that it was broad daylight and Saul lived on a dead-end road in a town so small that everything was fodder for the local gossip. Paul supposed if he got caught poking around, he'd claim to have been sent to the wrong place looking for a fishing hole. It was as believable as anything else that was going on in Johnson's Bayou.

"House" was an ambitious term for the shack that emerged at the end of the bumpy dirt road. For a man who made his living doing maintenance and repair, Saul Pritchard apparently didn't bother to take any time for his own structure. One end of the porch sagged so low it covered part of a window behind it, and tin patching dotted the roof where shingles were likely missing beneath.

Paul parked his truck and tucked his pistol in his waistband before getting out. According to his partner's research, Saul lived alone, but you never knew how accurate that was with bayou inhabitants. Sometimes extended families shared homes with only one person's name on everything. Money was often scarce in these parts.

He approached the house carefully, ready to turn and flee if shots were fired, but only silence met his approach. He hesitated a moment before stepping onto the porch, wondering if the rotted boards would hold his weight. The last thing he needed was to get a leg stuck out here and be unable to get free. That might look suspicious to even the most cavalier of people.

The boards groaned and sagged as he took the first step, but they held. He let out a breath of relief and edged toward the grimy window next to the door. Peering inside, he scanned the cluttered, dusty room filled with torn, damaged furniture and stacked high with newspapers, half-filled boxes and at least three cats.

After reviewing Saul's bank records, Paul's partner had reported that he regularly removed a hunk of cash from the account where he received the mysterious deposits, but darned if Paul could see where he was spending it. Likely, he had a drinking, drug or gambling problem and the money got funneled into the New Orleans system during a weekend bender.

He knew he should leave. There was nothing here to see but the sad cabin of a disgruntled man, but he found himself testing the doorknob. He was surprised when it turned easily and the door popped open. One of the cats jumped off the couch and onto a stack of newspaper, sending it scattering across the littered floor. At the same time, a group of small birds hiding in a bush behind him decided the cat was too close and burst from the bush, leaving a shower of leaves in their wake.

Paul spun around when the birds burst out of the bush, his pulse racing. When he realized it was the birds and not someone sneaking up behind him, he blew out a breath. This was stupid. He glanced back at the open door. But what if there was proof inside that Saul was Ginny's attacker? Granted, it wouldn't be admissible in court if he took anything out of the house, but he may be able to make a big enough stink to get the sheriff to get a search warrant, if for no other reason than to make Paul go away.

Before the sane part of his brain could talk him out of it, he stepped inside and closed the door behind him. If anyone caught him, he'd come up with a story appropriate to fool whoever did the catching.

The shack was essentially one big room with a living area, kitchenette and a sort of bedroom, which consisted of a mattress and box spring stacked on the floor in the far corner. Paul stepped through the tiny room, scanning the paper on the floor and furniture for anything of interest, but it appeared to be mostly old newspaper.

How does someone live like this? Especially when they don't have to.

Twenty-five thousand a year wasn't wealthy standards, but that cashier's check along with whatever he made contracting could have afforded Saul a much better lifestyle than this. He stepped into the kitchen and pulled open the refrigerator door, expecting it to be full of beer, but it was empty. He started to close it then realized that no cold air had blasted out when he'd opened the door.

Paul had no idea really why he bothered to look behind the refrigerator to see if it was plugged in, but he was glad he did. There was no outlet at all on the wall, which was really odd because the kitchen cabinets fit around the refrigerator in the slot where it rested. Clearly, it was intended to be placed in this spot.

He scanned the wall again, certain he must have missed the outlet, and that's when he noticed a tiny gap in the paneling. The refrigerator was an old model but still on wheels, and he easily pulled it forward to get a better look at the wall. He ran his finger down the crack between two pieces of paneling, then knocked on one of them.

It was hollow!

He gave the panel a shove and it opened wide, exposing a staircase. Nothing in the world could have stopped him from going down the staircase. Curiosity with just a tinge of fear overwhelmed him as he crept down, the light fading with every step. At the bottom of the staircase, the wall in front of him ended. Using his hands as a guide, he determined that there was an opening to the right.

Reaching around the corner of the opening, he ran his hand up and down the wall until he finally connected with a light switch. He paused for just a second, every possibility of what he might see flashing through his mind, and none of them good. Taking a deep breath, he flipped the switch.

And stared at the one thing he never, ever expected to see.

Chapter Fifteen

Ginny and Madelaine were stacking the boxes of café items in a corner of the kitchen when a knock sounded on the front door of the café. They stared at each other, frozen, for a minute, and Ginny knew they were both thinking that it was far too soon for Paul to return. He'd left only twenty minutes before, and Ginny had filled her mother in on Paul's plan to scout out Saul's house as soon as they'd gotten out of the contractor's earshot.

Finally, Madelaine shook her head. "We're letting ourselves get spooked." She left the kitchen to see who was knocking.

Ginny watched as she walked through the doors to the café. Madelaine was right. They were all on edge… jumpy and suspicious. Ginny even more so after last night. The dream was bad enough, frightening enough to make her jumpy, but what weighed on her even more was making love to Paul.

She'd completely lowered her guard with him, responding in ways she'd never felt with another man—taking in the whole of him, body, mind and spirit. It had been exciting and passionate and a rush like nothing else she'd ever experienced.

And that scared her even more than the nightmare.

Paul wasn't a local and wasn't going to become one. Once he was satisfied that Ginny was safe, he'd head back to his regular life in New Orleans and reconnect with his sister. Even if Ginny were willing to move to the city, what was the point? Paul had never so much as suggested that what was between them was a relationship or a precursor to one.

And she didn't blame him.

Anyone could take one look at her and know she wasn't the kind of woman who took risks and certainly wasn't the kind of person who had to have answers. All these years living a stone's throw from that relic of a school and she'd never once wanted to know what happened—where she came from and why. She'd just accepted what was.

Or maybe she'd been too afraid of the answers she might find.

Paul was anything but a coward, and he deserved someone in his life who could meet him with the same level of energy and enthusiasm he had. Ginny was orderly and routine and relished simplicity. She wasn't the woman for Paul.

"Ginny." Madelaine's voice broke into her thoughts and she looked up as her mother stepped into the kitchen followed by Sheriff Blackwell.

Instantly, Ginny's thoughts flashed to Paul's plan to search Saul's house. "Is anything wrong?"

"No," he reassured her. "I was just stopping to check in and give you an update."

"You found something?"

The sheriff shook his head. "I'm sorry. There wasn't a bit of evidence at your mom's house, and

I've been unable to track down any of the missing four-wheelers." He looked as frustrated as Ginny felt.

"That's okay," she said. "I know you're doing everything you can, especially with nothing to go on."

Madelaine nodded. "Ginny's absolutely right. Don't let Mayor Daigle and his blustering agitate you. Everyone knows the man's a windbag."

Sheriff Blackwell narrowed his eyes at Madelaine. "When did you talk to Mayor Daigle?"

Madelaine frowned. "He stopped by here earlier, telling us how sorry he was and how he'd read you the riot act for not calling him up personally. I guess so he could do nothing."

Sheriff Blackwell's face was blank, but Ginny saw his jaw twitch and knew he wasn't happy. She wasn't aware of any animosity between the two men, but now that she thought about it, they didn't seem to spend much time in each other's company.

"Are you taking any precautions?" he asked. "On the off-chance that this wasn't random?"

Madelaine nodded. "Paul's gone to buy new locks for the café and my house right now, and he's got a friend who's pricing a security system for me."

The sheriff nodded. "Times are changing. A security system's a good idea."

He looked over at Ginny, and she got the impression that he was studying her for something, but she had no idea what. Sanity, maybe? He must have been satisfied with what he saw, because finally he pulled his keys out of his pocket.

"Looks like you've got everything handled here," he said. "I'll get out of your way. You let me know if you have any more trouble."

Madelaine followed the sheriff out of the kitchen to let him out of the café, then returned a minute later, wearing a frown. Ginny took one look at her and realized that her mother was just as bothered by the sheriff's visit as she was, but the frown disappeared as soon as she realized Ginny was looking at her. Which could only mean one thing—Madelaine was hiding something to "protect" her.

"That was a little strange," Ginny said, determined to get at whatever Madelaine was holding back.

Madelaine turned her back to Ginny and busied herself rearranging pots on the counter. "He was just checking in."

"With nothing? More like he was trying to see if I was running with scissors or talking to myself. I saw him studying me. He still thinks I imagined the entire thing."

Madelaine sighed. "Maybe he does. But he's a stubborn, prideful man. He'll do his job and look into it, even if he doesn't believe there's anything to find. Maybe he'll surprise us and come up with something that blows the lid off the entire mess."

"It doesn't bother you—what people might think?"

An angry flush crept up Madelaine's neck. "It's never once bothered me when people are wrong, and I'm not about to start letting it now. Time will tell who's crazy in this town, but the one thing I'm certain about is it's not you."

Ginny smiled. Madelaine always had a way of making her feel protected and loved and, most important, normal. "So why the question about taking precautions?" Ginny mused. "Why the enthusiasm over locks and a security system if he's so sure there's nothing going on?"

Madelaine shook her head. "Maybe he's just hedging his bets in case he's wrong. Then if something happens he can at least say he followed up and suggested extra security precautions."

"Maybe. Or maybe he knows something he's not telling us. Something that makes him think there's that slight chance I may be telling the truth."

PAUL WAVED TO THE CLERK sweeping the sidewalk in front of the hardware store as he jumped in his truck with the bag of locks. He'd made sure to spread the word about his project and had no doubt that within minutes, residents of Johnson's Bayou would begin to gossip that the young stranger was changing locks for the café owner and her single daughter.

But all Paul could think about was what he'd found in Saul's house. He had no idea what to make of it and couldn't wait to get back to the café and tell Ginny and Madelaine what he'd found. His cell phone rang and he glanced at the display.

Unknown caller.

He frowned and answered the call.

"It's Kathy."

Paul clenched the phone as soon as he heard the anxiety in her voice. "What's wrong? Are you calling me from somewhere safe?"

"Yes. I'm at a friend's house watching her kids while she goes to the doctor. I know you said not to contact you until you let us know it's safe, but I had to talk to you."

"Has something happened?"

"I had a dream last night…a horrible nightmare. I woke up screaming and scared John half to death. He's beside himself with worry, but I don't know what to do about it."

"Can you remember the dreams?"

"Some, but it's not complete. I remember flashes but not the whole."

Paul reached for his pad of paper and pen in his glove box. "Tell me what you remember."

"I'm sitting in a dark place. There are boxes surrounding me and just a crack of light, like a crack in a door. I'm peering through it and there are two people arguing—a man and a lady. He's yelling at her, but I can't remember the words."

"Can you describe them?"

"Something is hanging down from the ceiling and blocking them from the waist up. She's wearing a long black skirt and high-heeled shoes. He's wearing black slacks and black dress shoes."

"Are you hiding somewhere, or did someone put you there?"

"I'm not sure, but it feels like I'm hiding. In the dream, I'm scared of being caught."

"Is there anything else you remember?"

"Yes. I have a pad of paper and I'm writing on it. There's a drawing, with circles, and then words, but I can't read what they say. Then the dream shifts and I'm peering into a dark room. Girls are huddled on the floor in the center of the room surrounded by a ring of burning candles. Just outside the ring is a table.

"I'm staring at the table," she continued. "I know I'm terrified, but I don't know why. Then someone in a black robe grabs one of the girls from inside the circle and I start to scream. And that's when I woke up, screaming, just like in my dream."

Paul felt the hair rise on the back of his neck as his sister described her dream. No way did two different women share the same fictional nightmare. It wasn't a bad dream—they were remembering. On the same night, no less.

"What do you think it all means?"

"I don't know," Paul replied, not wanting to frighten Kathy any more than she already was before he understood more of what was happening.

"Has Ginny had dreams?"

"Just once that I'm aware of." He could still remember her eyes, wide with fright, her body drenched in sweat, and the scream…as if someone were torturing her. Suddenly a thought occurred to him, so odd and unnatural that he almost didn't ask, but he had to know. "Out of curiosity—what time did you have the dream?"

"When I looked at the clock it was two minutes past midnight."

The same time Ginny had awakened screaming.

MADELAINE, GINNY AND PAUL regrouped in Ginny's apartment when he returned to the café in order to avoid being overheard. Ginny could tell that Paul had something important to tell them simply by the amount of nervous energy rolling off of him. The energy was infectious and Ginny found herself hurrying her mother, who was ironing the new tablecloths, to drop everything and get upstairs.

Paul had barely closed the apartment door behind them when Ginny said, "You found something."

"I found a whole lot of something."

He told them about finding Saul's shack and the mess he saw when peeking inside, then his discovery that the door was unlocked and his decision to look inside. When he described the refrigerator covering the hidden stairwell, both Madelaine and Ginny gasped.

"What was down there?" Ginny asked, afraid to imagine what he'd found in the hidden basement.

"You're not going to believe it," Paul said, shaking his head in obvious disbelief. "It was a huge room— easily twice as big as the shack above it—completely furnished with top-of-the-line everything. Leather furniture, an enormous big-screen television, hundreds of DVDs, a gourmet kitchen…it looked like a fancy penthouse apartment."

Ginny stared at Paul, her jaw dropping. Of all the things in the world she'd thought she may hear, this was so far out of the realm that she was stunned silent. She looked over at Madelaine, who stared at Paul in complete disbelief.

Paul pulled out his cell phone and showed them the pictures he'd taken in Saul's basement. They gasped as he scrolled through something so far removed from what they'd imagined the man's house to possess.

"You're right," Madelaine said finally, "I wouldn't believe it if you weren't standing there saying it and showing us those pictures. What in the world…it boggles the mind."

"So he gets money from some mysterious source that can't be traced," Ginny said, "and instead of moving or building a nicer house, he constructs a luxury basement. Why?"

Paul shook his head. "I've rolled a million ideas

around in my head, but not a one of them answers that question to any satisfaction. But then, given the strangeness of the person in question, who knows?"

Paul hesitated for a moment, glancing from Madelaine to Ginny before continuing. "I found something else in the storage shed out back—an ATV. With a bullet hole in the tank."

Ginny sucked in a breath and Madelaine brought one hand up to cover her mouth. "It *was* him," Ginny said.

"Given the four-wheeler and the unaccounted-for deposits, it doesn't look good," Paul said. "But we can't be certain. Someone else could have used the ATV. The shed wasn't locked."

Madelaine narrowed her eyes at Paul. "Does someone pay him twenty-five-thousand a year to borrow that ATV? The man was being paid for something— be it taking action or keeping silent."

Paul nodded. "But which one?"

"I don't know," Madelaine said, "but I guess I better get downstairs and see what he's up to."

Madelaine shot Ginny a look as she closed the apartment door behind her, and Ginny knew her mother was giving her an opportunity to clear the tension between her and Paul. Ginny let out a sigh. She'd done an awful job of masking her emotional turmoil if Madelaine had picked up on it so easily, but then her mother had always been tuned to her. Maybe that was just how mothers were, DNA or no.

An uncomfortable silence settled in the apartment as Madelaine's footsteps faded away on the stairs. Ginny struggled to find the right way to open the conversation, to tell Paul that she understood why he wouldn't want a future with her and why she didn't blame him, but when she opened her mouth to speak, he spoke instead.

"Kathy called me."

Ginny felt her pulse quicken. "But you told her not to. Is something wrong?"

Paul sat on the couch and motioned for Ginny to join him. She perched on the edge of the couch next to him, certain he was about to tell her something she didn't want to hear.

"She had a dream last night—a nightmare—that freaked her out." Paul stared over Ginny's shoulder at the wall for a moment, then looked back at her. "Her dream was like yours, except like she'd seen it from a different angle, from inside the house instead of out-side."

Ginny sucked in a breath and felt her chest constrict. "How is that possible?"

"I think…I think maybe what you both dreamed is what actually happened. It explains why you dreamed it from a child's point of view, why you had similari-ties in your dream, and—"

"Why both of us are alive," Ginny finished for him. "We both hid and weren't in the room with the other girls. That's why we're alive."

Paul nodded and the compassion and caring that was so obvious in his delivery, in his expression, sent a single tear sliding down her cheek.

"How did we get away? Why didn't they know we weren't there?"

"I'm not sure, but I think you were both new. I think that's why neither of you remembers the other girls but you remembered the circles. Maybe you came to the school at the same time as my sister. Maybe when the man and woman realized you weren't in the room with the other girls, it didn't matter because you didn't know what they were covering up."

"They didn't know that we saw the girls die."

"Neither of you had any memory after being rescued. All these years and you haven't shown any signs of remembering."

"Until now."

Paul nodded.

"That means you were right—it's someone I know. The woman had to be the headmistress, but the man… that blurred face in my dreams is someone from Johnson's Bayou."

"I'm so sorry, Ginny. When I think about what you and Kathy went through…well, it makes sense that you forgot. It was your mind's way of saving you."

"What happened to them—the girls?"

Paul hesitated for a moment and Ginny knew he was going to tell her something unpleasant. "The description with the robe and mask, the black candles… it sounds like a cult."

Ginny sucked in a breath. "You think he was going to sacrifice that girl? That table was an altar?"

"I had Mike check and there were several cults under investigation in the New Orleans area at that time. They had factions in surrounding bayou towns. The LeBlanc School could have been a front for one of them."

"But what was going on at that school? All those girls and no one to claim them. I intentionally kept myself from thinking about it all these years. I'm a coward." Ginny stared down at the couch.

"You're not a coward," Paul said and placed his hand over hers. "You were surviving. And if you hadn't put it all out of your mind, he would have come after you before now. Before you were better prepared to deal with it."

Ginny gave him a small smile. "Before you were here to help me."

Paul squeezed her hand. "We're going to get through this, and then your life can be about the future and not the past."

The future.

Paul's words hung in the air as if to tease her with possibilities that she knew would never be. She raised her gaze to his and realized just how close to her he was. He leaned in to kiss her and her body responded before her mind could put on the brakes.

His lips had barely brushed her own when Paul's cell phone rang, sending Ginny springing up from the couch in a panic. What was she thinking? Why was she dragging this out when it would only hurt her in the end? She hurried into the bathroom, not even glancing back at Paul. Knowing that if she looked at him, the tears that were threatening to fall would spill over.

Chapter Sixteen

Paul jumped up from the couch after Ginny, pulling his phone from his pocket as he rose. He started to go after her, to stop her from avoiding the conversation they clearly needed to have, when he noticed the display.

It was Kathy's home phone number.

He answered the call, trying not to imagine why Kathy would ignore his warnings and call from her home.

"Kathy's gone!" John's frantic voice sounded over the phone. "I came home from work and the stove was on, but she's nowhere. Her car is in the driveway. Her purse is on the kitchen counter. But the police won't do a damned thing until she's been missing for twenty-four hours because there's no sign of forced entry. What the hell did you get us involved in?"

Paul's heart fell. This was exactly the situation he'd tried so hard to avoid. "I'm on my way," he said and pulled his keys from his jeans pocket.

Ginny stepped out of the bathroom, her worry apparent. "What's wrong?" she asked.

"Kathy's missing."

Ginny's hands flew up to cover her mouth. "Oh, no," she said as Paul checked the clip on his pistol then shoved it back in the waistband of his jeans. "I'm coming with you—and no arguing."

Paul closed his mouth, knowing words wouldn't make a bit of difference, and in reality, if Ginny was with him, he wouldn't have to worry about her. She grabbed her purse from the coffee table and they rushed downstairs, almost colliding with Madelaine, who was just starting up the stairs.

"What's wrong?" Madelaine asked.

Paul filled her in and Madelaine's eyes widened.

"He's gone," she said, her voice almost a whisper.

"Who's gone?" Paul asked.

"Saul. When I came back downstairs, he wasn't anywhere to be seen." She stared at Paul. "Do you think he could have crept upstairs and heard us?"

Paul struggled to control the panic threatening to break through. "I don't know, but we're going to find out." He looked directly at Madelaine. "I need you to lock the doors, open the front windows of the café and stay up there until we get back. No one will risk coming after you while you're window dressing—at least not in daylight."

Madelaine gave Ginny a quick hug. "Be careful."

PAUL MADE THE DRIVE to John and Kathy's house in twenty minutes flat, breaking at least five laws along the way. John was standing at the front door when they pulled up, and the look on his face broke Paul's heart all over again. His truck had barely come to a complete stop in the driveway before both of them jumped out and rushed inside.

"Tell me everything," Paul said as he took a seat at the dining table across from John. "Everything that's happened since my visit, even if it seems unimportant. I want to know everything you talked about that has to do with the past, everywhere Kathy's gone since then, every visitor she's had to the house…"

Ginny, who'd slipped into the kitchen as soon as they entered the house, walked into the dining room and placed a glass of water in front of John and poured a couple of aspirin from a bottle in her purse. He gave her a grateful look and popped the aspirin, then took a big gulp of water before he started to talk.

"She had a nightmare last night. Her entire body was ringing with sweat and she woke screaming. Then she called at lunch and told me she was having these 'spells,' as she called them. She said it was like seeing a picture album but with no rhyme or reason as to why."

Ginny nodded. "I think it's flashes of memory from the past. The same thing has been happening to me. What did she see?"

John nodded. "She said she saw an older woman with long, wiry black hair."

"The headmistress of the LeBlanc School," Ginny said.

"She saw a stack of curtains, blue with yellow flowers."

Ginny sucked in a breath. "Those are the curtains that used to hang at my mother's café. She bought them from the girls at the school." She went on to tell John about finding the note in the hem of the curtain.

John buried his head in his hands for a couple of seconds, and when he looked back up, the misery on his face was crystal clear. "What happened to her…to you? You were just little girls."

"I'm just speculating, but I don't think Kathy and Ginny were there very long before the fire," Paul said. "Whatever happened to the other girls before then, I'm not sure it happened to Kathy and Ginny."

A tiny bit of hope appeared on John's face, then it disappeared. "If nothing bad happened to them, then why did Kathy have such a terrible nightmare?"

"I think they saw the other girls being killed. Each of them hid when the others were being gathered, but I think both snuck back to see what was happening."

"So you're sure the fire was intentional?"

"I think it started when the girls panicked, but locking them in a room with no escape was intentional."

"Oh, my God." The agonizing look on John's face said it all.

"Is there anything else?" Paul asked.

John shook his head, then frowned. "I'm not sure this is part of the same thing, but it's starting to sound like it. It's been years—since college, actually—but Kathy used to sleepwalk. She'd be missing from the bed in the middle of the night and I'd go looking for her. The first time it happened, I was in an all-out panic because I couldn't find her, but when I started looking more thoroughly than just scanning the rooms, I found her in the pantry, sitting on the floor with a notebook and pencil."

"Was anything written on it?"

"Just some circles. No writing at all. She didn't know how she got in the closet or why she was there. It happened several times during college and then just stopped. I had almost forgotten until today."

"I guess I don't have to ask…" Paul began.

John shook his head. "I checked every closet first

thing. Checked the attic, the storage shed, everywhere a grown adult could fit, just in case. She's nowhere on this property."

"Could she have fallen asleep and wandered off during one of those nightmares?"

"I don't see how. I talked to her when I was leaving my office, which is only twenty minutes away. She said she was going to start dinner, and the stove was on when I got here. Why would she take a nap after turning on the stove?"

Paul looked over at Ginny, who shook her head, a grave look on her face. They had to assume the killer had Kathy. At this point, there was no other logical explanation.

"Where is she?" John asked. "Surely, you have some idea. You've been working on this." The desperation in John's voice was heartbreaking.

Paul slowly shook his head, gazing out the window into the backyard. Then suddenly, a thought occurred to him. "Maybe the question we should be asking is 'why' and not 'where.'"

"What do you mean?" Ginny asked.

"When the man attacked you at your mother's house, he had a gun. He could have killed you there. We have to assume that if he has Kathy, he had the same opportunity to kill her here, in her own home. So why didn't he? Instead, he hit you on the back of the head—something you do if you want someone unconscious."

John's eyes widened. "He wanted to take them somewhere."

"The school," Ginny whispered. "It has to be the school."

"But why?" John asked.

Paul's jaw flexed and then set in a hard line. "Because then he could make their deaths look like an accident or suicide. Both of them came from the school with no past and serious medical issues once rescued."

"People would think we went insane," Ginny said, "because of the past."

John jumped up from the table. "We have to go get her!"

Paul rose and placed one hand on John's arm. "I want to find Kathy as badly as you, but I need you to go to the police department and tell them your wife was kidnapped. Tell them you received a frantic phone call and that she's being held hostage at the old LeBlanc School for Girls in Johnson's Bayou."

John stared. "You want me to lie to the police?"

"Yes. Otherwise, they won't take you seriously. It will still take them some time to get moving, but if you threaten to go yourself, they'll send someone. I may need backup. I'm counting on you, John."

John didn't look happy with the situation at all, but finally he nodded. "Okay. I'll go now and raise hell until they send someone, but I'm going with them."

"I don't blame you," Paul said.

As he and Ginny started to leave the house, John grabbed Paul's arm. "Find my wife. Bring her back to me."

"I intend to," Paul said before they rushed outside and jumped into Paul's truck.

Paul floored the accelerator and the truck tires squealed as they slid onto the road. He punched in his partner's number on the cell phone and gave him a quick rundown of the situation and asked for backup.

Mike was more than an hour away from Johnson's Bayou, but Paul wanted someone who'd been involved from the beginning to know what they were doing.

When Paul finished the call to his partner, he glanced over at Ginny, who sat stock-still, clutching the seat with both hands. "We're going to find her," Paul said. "We're going to end this."

Ginny nodded, but the fear on her face was evident.

Paul's own heart raced so hard he could feel it pulsing through his fingers as he gripped the steering wheel. The rest of the drive to Johnson's Bayou was made in complete silence, and Paul knew both of them were running a list of possible outcomes through their minds. He parked in front of the café and Madelaine was already at the front door, ushering them inside.

"Grab your spotlight," Paul told Ginny. "It will be dark soon."

Paul filled Madelaine in on what happened and his theory as Ginny raced upstairs to grab the light. When Ginny rushed back down seconds later, Madelaine pulled her rifle from underneath the counter.

"Let's go," Madelaine said. "And don't even try to talk me out of it. He may have been able to pull off killing Ginny and Kathy and making it look like suicide, but he can't kill all of us without bringing down the house of cards."

Paul didn't even waste time arguing with her. She'd just follow them anyway, and he wanted to get to the school as soon as possible. Besides, if Madelaine was half the shot she claimed to be, he may need her. "Both of you do exactly as I say. Follow close behind and try not to talk. If you hear or see something, touch me and point. Got it?"

Ginny and Madelaine nodded.

They left the café by the back door and hurried across the field to the swamp, entering the dense brush at the same place Paul and Ginny had before. Madelaine huffed behind them but surprised Paul when she didn't lag. The look of determination and anger on her face explained it, though. Someone was threatening her child and adrenaline had kicked in.

Paul pushed through the brush as fast as he could, trying to keep the noise level to a minimum, but he knew if the killer was within hearing distance, he'd recognize the sounds of something large approaching. Assuming he was from Johnson's Bayou, he'd know the difference between the local creatures and humans.

In other words, he'd be ready for them.

GINNY FOLLOWED PAUL into the ever-darkening swamp, her heart beating faster with each step. Her mind raced with all the bad possibilities of what might be happening to Kathy, and she shook her head to stop the barrage of frightful images.

Kathy will be all right. She just had to keep telling herself that.

She didn't realize Paul had stopped until she bumped into him. Peering around him, she realized they had reached the edge of the school grounds. Paul scanned the grounds, and Ginny knew he was assessing the best entry point.

Finally, he turned to them and whispered, "We'll skirt the edge of the grounds until we reach the storage shed on the side. There's only one window upstairs on that side of the house that has a clear view over the shed and into the swamp. It gives us the best coverage to approach the house without being seen. We can go in the side door at the kitchen."

Ginny and Madelaine nodded before dropping into step behind Paul as they skirted their way around the school grounds along the edge of the swamp. When they reached the section of the swamp closest to the storage shed Paul stopped and scanned the grounds again then motioned to them to follow him as he crept out of the swamp toward the storage shed.

Ginny and Madelaine followed behind him single file then pressed their backs against the shed. Paul peeked around the end of the shed, then waved at them to follow, and they moved silently from behind the shed into the house. Paul stopped just inside the kitchen and put a finger to his lips. He stood completely motionless, trying to pinpoint the existence of any other humans in the house. All Ginny heard was the sound of her own heartbeat.

Paul leaned in and whispered, "I think we should check the room that caught fire first."

Ginny nodded. If the killer was trying to make Kathy's death look like a suicide, the scene of the tragedy was the most logical to choose. Unfortunately, it was also down a long hallway at the other end of the house. They were going to have to be very deliberate with every step. Even the smallest noise would echo throughout the cavernous house.

Silently, they slipped down the hall, carefully choosing their steps to avoid anything on the littered floor that would make a noise. At the end of the hall stood what was left of the burned room. The door was closed and Ginny held her breath as Paul turned the knob and inched the door open. She let the breath out when the hinges didn't screech and followed Paul through the small opening he'd created into the room.

It took only a quick scan to know they were completely alone. Decades of old ash and dust coated every surface in the room, including the floor. No one had been in this room in years, much less today.

Disappointment and anxiety washed over Ginny as they crept back into the hall. What if they'd been wrong? What if Kathy was somewhere else and they were wasting valuable time looking for her here? And then she remembered John's story of Kathy's sleepwalking. It was a huge long shot, but something she had to try.

She motioned to Paul and Madelaine and made her way back down the hallway to the kitchen. Once inside, she eased the hallway door shut behind them, knowing that it would prevent some sound in the room from being carried into the hall and the entryway. She pointed at the pantry, and Paul's eyes widened.

He eased the door open and sitting on the floor of the pantry, staring wide-eyed at them, was a very alive Kathy. She gasped when she saw them and scrambled from the closet on her hands and knees. Paul reached a hand down to help her up, and she rose and threw her arms around him, choking back a sob.

Finally, she broke away, her eyes darting around the room. "The man who took me—where is he?" she whispered.

Paul shook his head. "Did he leave you here?"

"No. I broke free in the swamp and ran. I found the school and hid here, but I heard him walking upstairs about ten minutes ago. He's looking for me."

"Did you recognize him?"

Kathy nodded. "He's the man from my dreams. The man who killed those girls. I've seen him somewhere before, but seeing him didn't mean anything to me then. I still don't know who he is now." She pointed to the pantry. "That's where I hid that night I heard him arguing with the woman. I didn't realize it until I was in there, hiding all over again."

Ginny placed her hand on Paul's arm. As much as she wanted answers, they needed to put off conversation until later. "We've got to get out of here before he comes back," she whispered.

Madelaine nodded, her eyes wide.

"You're right," Paul agreed. "We'll leave the same way we came. I'll lead and Madelaine, you come last with the rifle."

Madelaine took her place behind Ginny and Kathy, and they eased through the back door and hurried to the back of the shed. Once there, they paused only long enough for Paul to scan the swamp and then they ran, but before they made it to the deep underbrush, Mayor Daigle stepped out with a pistol leveled directly at them.

"Drop your weapon," he said to Paul. "Madelaine, toss that rifle this way, and no tricks, or beautiful Ginny gets a bullet."

Ginny gasped. "It was you. All this time, it was you."

"Real estate," Paul said, cursing himself for not making the connection sooner. "Your wife's family has a real estate trust. That trust owned the café before Madelaine bought it. That's how you had access to the café, which gave you access to the keys to Ginny's apartment and Madelaine's house that she kept in her desk drawer. You got the key to the café from the estate attorney, and since everything is held in the trust's name, no one ever connected you with the building."

"Smart boy," Mayor Daigle said and motioned to Paul's gun again. "But not smart enough, apparently."

Paul dropped his pistol and Madelaine followed suit with her rifle. Mayor Daigle waved his pistol at them, motioning them back toward the house. "It didn't have to be this way," he said. "If only you hadn't started to remember. But I just can't take the chance. Not when I'm so close to everything I wanted."

"You can't kill us all without bringing down an investigation," Paul said.

"Sure I can. You see, Kathy and Ginny here couldn't take the memories haunting them anymore, so they came to the house to get 'closure.' That's popular these days. But instead, being here drove them over the edge, and when you and Madelaine showed up looking for them, they killed you and then themselves, but not before setting fire to the house one last time."

"Why?" Ginny asked. "Why did you kill those girls?"

Mayor Daigle shook his head. "Because they knew too much and the job was over. Now, I want all of you to turn slowly and walk back into the kitchen. I'll make this quick, as I have a speaking engagement tonight."

The bushes behind the mayor rustled and Sheriff Blackwell stepped out, a shotgun trained on the mayor's head. "I'm sorry, Joe, but I can't let you do that."

Mayor Daigle sighed. "You don't want to do this, or you're going down with me."

"I deserve to," Sheriff Blackwell said. "I should have turned you in back then."

Instead of replying, Mayor Daigle spun around and knocked Sheriff Blackwell's shotgun with one hand while firing his pistol with the other. Paul and Madelaine lunged for their guns at the same time as Mayor Daigle grabbed Ginny and pushed his pistol into her temple.

Mayor Daigle glanced over at the prone body of Sheriff Blackwell and laughed. "Let's try this again, shall we? You two, drop your weapons and get into that house before any more heroes show up."

Ginny looked at her mother's tear-streaked face, at Kathy, who looked on the verge of collapse, and then at Paul. There were so many things she wished she had time to say. So many things she wished she would have said before. To hell with the future. She should have told him how she felt when she had the chance, regardless of how it might have turned out. At least he would have known.

He stared at her now with stark fear in his eyes, and she knew he was preparing for the worst. Once they were inside, it would be over. No more chances to right the past. No more chances to tell him how she felt. And for Ginny, that wasn't good enough. She was already dead, so taking one last chance wasn't really taking a chance at all.

She looked straight at him and winked. His eyes widened slightly just as she slumped to the ground as if unconscious. The instant deadweight caught Mayor Daigle by surprise, and he dropped her as she collapsed. Without a second of hesitation, Paul dove for his pistol and fired a single killing shot through Mayor Daigle's head before the man could even register what was happening.

Paul dropped to the ground and gathered Ginny in his arms. "I thought I'd lost you," he murmured. "You took such a risk…"

"I had to." She pushed back a bit so that she could look at him. "It was the only way to get another chance. I had to tell you I loved you."

"Oh, Ginny," Paul said and lowered his lips to hers in a gentle kiss. "I felt guilty for all the upheaval I brought into your life. I know you'd already set things in motion before I arrived, but I couldn't help feeling responsible. But now that it's over I have to tell you that I love you, Ginny, and I'm going to keep telling you until you're tired of hearing it."

"I'll never get tired," Ginny said.

They rose from the ground and Madelaine rushed to hug both of them. Paul extended his hand to Kathy, who joined them.

A groan sounded nearby and they immediately broke apart, Madelaine and Paul readying their weapons.

"Sheriff Blackwell," Madelaine said and hurried over to where the sheriff was holding his hand against his side, blood seeping through his fingers.

Ginny pulled off her light jacket and handed it to Madelaine, who pressed it into the sheriff's side, trying to stop the blood loss. "Don't bother," he gasped. "It's too late for me, but I have to tell you I'm sorry."

"What was happening at the school that the mayor covered up?" Paul asked.

"Child pornography. He had cameras set up in all the girls' rooms and the shower areas. He and that woman were selling the tapes overseas for a huge profit."

"How did you find out?"

"I caught him loading cardboard boxes into his car at the school after the fire. He was real skittish and never answered me when I asked what he was hauling away. I followed him to a warehouse in New Orleans and as he was carrying the boxes inside, I sneaked to his car and saw the box of tapes. I took one with me and watched."

Ginny felt the blood wash from her face. "Oh, no. They were being abused."

Sheriff Blackwell shook his head. "I never saw anything like that on the tape, but there was no mistaking what those tapes were meant to be. I suppose given enough time, the abuse would have started."

"I always felt like someone was watching me," Kathy said. "No wonder."

"Why didn't you turn him in?" Madelaine asked. "I know you, Thomas. You would never condone something like this."

"He took money," Paul said. "Mayor Daigle bought your silence."

Sheriff Blackwell looked directly at them, his eyes filled with shame. "I swear, I didn't know anything about the tapes until after the fire, and until I overheard Daigle confess today, I didn't know for certain that they'd locked those girls in to die. I'd caught the occult overtones and thought maybe it was a ritual gone wrong. I guess that's what we were all supposed to think.

"You have to understand," Sheriff Blackwell said. "Those girls were already dead, but my Meg wasn't."

Madelaine gasped. "You took money from Daigle

for Meg's cancer treatments. The ones that insurance wouldn't pay for."

Sheriff Blackwell nodded. "She was in so much pain. I made him promise me that he'd never bother Ginny or Kathy. I've watched closely all these years, and he kept his promise."

"Until now," Paul said, "but you covered for him again by pretending you thought Ginny had imagined her attack. You knew it was him."

"I thought I could convince him to leave it alone. I thought he'd believe that they weren't remembering."

"Do you know where the girls came from?"

"Daigle said some were wards of the state with no family to speak of. The headmistress gave couples false identities and paid them to foster the kids and turn them over to her. Others they bought from desperate, poor bayou families, probably promising that their babies would have a good life with a wealthy family."

"Who was the headmistress and what happened to her?" Ginny asked.

"I don't know how Daigle met her, but she's dead. It looked like a random carjacking, but I've always wondered." He put his hand up to his mouth and coughed, and when he lowered it, Ginny could see it was covered with blood.

"The tape is locked in my safe," Sheriff Blackwell said. "Take it and expose all of this. It's long overdue." He looked at Ginny and Kathy. "I'm sorry I never stood up for you when it mattered. I hope one day you can forgive me." He coughed again and his body locked, almost as if in seizure, then everything relaxed and he collapsed on the ground.

Paul felt his neck and shook his head. "He's dead."

Madelaine looked down at him and sighed. "He always said he would have done anything to save Meg. I guess he did. It must have eaten him up all these years." She put one arm around Ginny and Kathy and squeezed. "But it all ends here, today."

Ginny smiled and reached out to take Paul's hand. "And a new life begins."

Epilogue

Six months later.

Ginny stuffed the last of the boxes in the back of her car and pushed the hatchback down until it barely clicked in place. She turned to face her mother, who stood with her outside the café, her eyes brimming with unshed tears.

"Are you sure this is what you want?" Madelaine asked.

Ginny smiled. "Look at you. You've pushed me for years to expand my horizons and then when I do, you're all tentative and sentimental." She gave her mother a hug. "I want to be with Paul. The past six months have been incredible. I want a whole lifetime of that, and I know I can have it with him."

"I know you will. I'm just used to seeing you every day, and now everything is different. You'll be attending college and making jewelry for all those stores in New Orleans, and you'll be spending the rest of your time with the man you love."

A tear rolled out of Madelaine's eye and down her cheek. She brushed it away with her hand and said, "I don't think I have to say how happy I am for you.

You're a wonderful woman, Ginny, and the best daughter a mother could ever have."

"And you're the best mother."

"Did Paul…was he ever able to find out anything…"

"No. I still don't have any idea where I came from, but I don't care. I've asked him to stop looking. I want to put the past behind me and focus on the future."

"And Kathy?"

"Is doing great. In fact, she called last night to say they're expecting their first baby."

Madelaine's face lit up. "Oh, that's wonderful to hear."

Paul stepped out of the café with a bag of pies that Madelaine had given him earlier. He placed the pies in the backseat of the car and walked over to give Madelaine a hug. "Don't worry about missing her," he said. "We'll be back to visit soon. After all, Ginny has a wedding to plan."

"Me?" Ginny pretended to slug him in the arm. "You are fifty percent responsible for all planning."

Paul wrapped his arms around her and kissed her gently and slowly. "Then I think we should elope. Tonight. And preferably to one of those places that doesn't require clothes."

Madelaine laughed. "Go on, you two. Get out of here."

Paul released Ginny and gave Madelaine a hug. "The café looks great, by the way. The new colors are really nice."

Ginny grinned. "And it only took Saul three weeks to finish the painting. A new record."

"Hey," Paul said, "did you ever find out where he went that day that we all went to the school?"

Madelaine shook her head. "Yeah. Someone came by and told him there was two-for-one steaks at the butcher. Apparently he bought enough for a small country. Probably got it stashed in that penthouse basement of his."

Ginny looked over at Paul. "Did you ever find out who gives him the money? I mean, I know he wasn't the bad guy and there was no reason to check into it, but I was just curious."

Paul smiled. "So was I, so I looked into it some more. Turns out our friend Mr. Pritchard won a lottery sixteen years ago. Apparently, he was afraid of being hit up for money from his lazy relatives, so he set the whole thing up with a trust to make annual payments by cashier's check."

"Unbelievable," Madelaine said. "Who would have ever believed that so many secrets could be contained in such a small place?"

Paul looked at Ginny. "Are you ready?" The question was so simple, but Ginny knew all the implications behind it.

She placed her hand in his and smiled. "You know it."

* * * * *

SUSPENSE

Heartstopping stories of intrigue and mystery—
where true love always triumphs.

 Harlequin

INTRIGUE

COMING NEXT MONTH
AVAILABLE MARCH 13, 2012

#1335 CORRALLED
Whitehorse, Montana:
Chisholm Cattle Company
B.J. Daniels

#1336 COWBOY TO THE MAX
Bucking Bronc Lodge
Rita Herron

#1337 SECRET IDENTITY
Cooper Security
Paula Graves

#1338 LAWMAN LOVER
Outlaws
Lisa Childs

#1339 A WANTED MAN
Thriller
Alana Matthews

#1340 FINDING HER SON
Robin Perini

You can find more information on upcoming Harlequin® titles,
free excerpts and more at www.HarlequinInsideRomance.com.

HICNM0212

REQUEST YOUR FREE BOOKS!
2 FREE NOVELS PLUS 2 FREE GIFTS!

Harlequin
INTRIGUE
BREATHTAKING ROMANTIC SUSPENSE

New York Times *and* USA TODAY *bestselling author Maya Banks presents book three in her miniseries* PREGNANCY & PASSION.

TEMPTED BY HER INNOCENT KISS

Available March 2012 from Harlequin Desire!

There came a time in a man's life when he knew he was well and truly caught. Devon Carter stared down at the diamond ring nestled in velvet and acknowledged that this was one such time. He snapped the lid closed and shoved the box into the breast pocket of his suit.

He had two choices. He could marry Ashley Copeland and fulfill his goal of merging his company with Copeland Hotels, thus creating the largest, most exclusive line of resorts in the world, or he could refuse and lose it all.

Put in that light, there wasn't much he could do except pop the question.

The doorman to his Manhattan high-rise apartment hurried to open the door as Devon strode toward the street. He took a deep breath before ducking into his car, and the driver pulled into traffic.

Tonight was the night. All of his careful wooing, the countless dinners, kisses that started brief and casual and became more breathless—all a lead-up to tonight. Tonight his seduction of Ashley Copeland would be complete, and then he'd ask her to marry him.

He shook his head as the absurdity of the situation hit him for the hundredth time. Personally, he thought William Copeland was crazy for forcing his daughter down Devon's throat.

Ashley was a sweet enough girl, but Devon had no desire

to marry anyone.

William had other plans. He'd told Devon that Ashley had no head for the family business. She was too softhearted, too naive. So he'd made Ashley part of the deal. The catch? Ashley wasn't to know of it. Which meant Devon was stuck playing stupid games.

Ashley was supposed to think this was a grand love match. She was a starry-eyed woman who preferred her animal-rescue foundation over board meetings, charts and financials for Copeland Hotels.

If she ever found out the truth, she wouldn't take it well.

And hell, he couldn't blame her.

But no matter the reason for his proposal, before the night was over, she'd have no doubts that she belonged to him.

What will happen when Devon marries Ashley?
Find out in Maya Banks's passionate new novel
TEMPTED BY HER INNOCENT KISS
Available March 2012 from Harlequin Desire!